Samuel French Acting Edition

One Toe in the Grave

by Jack Sharkey

I0591866

‖SAMUEL FRENCH‖

SAMUELFRENCH.COM **SAMUELFRENCH.CO.UK**

Please refer to page 99 for further copyright information.

CAST OF CHARACTERS

JASON KINGSLEY, a rising young business executive
MONICA (a.k.a. NICKI) CHANNING, his bride-to-be
NAOMI SCHUYLER, Jason's longtime housekeeper
THORNTON MURDOCK, Jason's spit-and-polish boss
DOUGLAS PROCTER, a corporate medical examiner
POOPSIE MAGRUDER, a young lady of 20 [age and IQ]

and

VONGA, The Jungle Girl

TIME: The present, during a *very* hot July
LOCALE: Jason's apartment in Manhattan

ACT ONE: Friday afternoon about 6 o'clock
ACT TWO: Immediately following
ACT THREE: About 15 minutes later

For
MORT SERTNER
a truly *great*
comedic "heavy"

One Toe in the Grave

ACT ONE

The Manhattan apartment of JASON KINGSLEY [see Set Design], about 6 p.m. on a Friday during a very hot July. At curtain-rise, stage is empty. Then DOORBELL RINGS, and NAOMI SCHUYLER enters into foyer from kitchen. NAOMI is a motherly woman in her 50s, and wears an apron over her dress. She opens front door and MONICA [a.k.a. NICKI] CHANNING, a young lady in her early 20s, strikingly lovely, rushes into foyer, her face aglow with happiness, carrying an overnight bag. Her manner is eager, slightly nervous, almost breathless.

NAOMI. (*amiable rather than formal*) Why, good evening, Miss Channing. Going on a trip?

NICKI. Didn't Jason tell you?

NAOMI. (*business of closing hall door*) Why *would* he? It's hardly any of *my* business.

NICKI. (*has moved down into living room and set suitcase just below R. railing*) But it *will* be when we get *back*, won't it? I mean, I just *assumed* you'd be staying *on*.

NAOMI. (*moving into living room after her, curious*) Get back from *where*? And what's this about my staying on? I've kept house for Mister Kingsley for three years, now. If I'm leaving, it's news to *me*.

NICKI. (*spins to face her*) Naomi, you *don't* know, do you! Jason and I are getting *married* tonight!

NAOMI. (*with a vague kitchenward gesture*) Then why am I fixing dinner for three?

5

NICKI. Dinner? For *three*? But — Jason said we'd be driving up to Connecticut the moment he got home from work!

NAOMI. It's a long drive. Maybe he thought you'd be hungry.

NICKI. Even so — who's the *third* person?

NAOMI. (*shrugs*) He didn't say . . . of course, *I* get hungry, too. Maybe he's including *me* in the prenuptial celebration. Which reminds me — congratulations!

NICKI. For what? *Oh*, you mean the wedding! Thank you, Naomi. But — are you *sure* about that dinner? Maybe he told you to fix it, and then after I accepted his proposal he was so excited he forgot to call you and cancel it.

NAOMI. Well, that's *possible*, I suppose. What time did he pop the question?

NICKI. (*with glow-eyed reminiscence*) At lunch! he was so romantic. I mean, he almost *never* drinks during business hours, but he ordered a bottle of wine, and —

NAOMI. Hold it. There's *something* screwy here . . . he called me about the dinner at three this afternoon! You *must* have finished eating by *then*!

NICKI. I was too *excited* to eat! So was Jason!

NAOMI. Then why am I fixing dinner for three? (*shrugs, starts toward* K.R.) Unless our Mystery Guest has a tapeworm. . . ?

NICKI. I guess we won't know till *Jason* gets here! (*DOORBELL*) Oh, there he is, now! (*starts for door*)

NAOMI. (*off*) Can't be. He has a key.

NICKI. (*almost at door*) Maybe it's our Mystery Guest! Should *I* get the door?

NAOMI. (*off*) Okay, but be careful!

NICKI. Why?

NAOMI. (*off*) I might be right about the *tapeworm*!

NICKI. (*wryly*) Really, Naomi!

NAOMI. (*off*) Just don't offer him your *hand*!

NICKI. (*laughs, opens door; DOUGLAS PROCTER, a young man in his early 30s, in sportcoat and open-necked shirt, looking distraught, rushes in*) Douglas! What are *you* doing here?!

DOUG. (*clutches her hands urgently*) Oh, Nicki, I *had* to come! I couldn't stand by and let you *do* this to yourself!

NICKI. (*pulls free of his hands, backs into living room*) Do *what*, Douglas? What are you *talking* about?

DOUG. (*absently shuts door, moves after her*) Oh, Nicki, when I think about it, I get cold chills — ! (*pauses, looks around*) At least, I *did* . . . Why is is so *hot* in here?

NAOMI. (*pokes head in via* K.L.) Mister Kingsley's orders. He said turn off the air-conditioning and start fixing dinner for three!

DOUG. In *July*? How could he *ask* such a thing of you?

NAOMI. I don't have a *union*.

NICKI. But *why* would he, Naomi?

NAOMI. Maybe our guest is from the Upper Amazon. (*exits* K.L.)

DOUG. *What* guest?

NICKI. We don't *know* yet, and don't change the subject! What are you *doing* here?!

DOUG. I saw you and Jason at lunch today! I overheard everything!

NICKI. Douglas! You were spying on us?

DOUG. Not intentionally. I was in the next booth. I recognized your voice!

NICKI. (*turns her back, folds her arms angrily*) A gentleman would have made his presence known!

Doug. I didn't want to embarrass you in public!

Nicki. (*whirs to face him, wide-eyed*) *Embarrass* me? *How?*

Doug. By punching Jason Kingsley in the nose!

Nicki. But why?!

Doug. (*shrugs, says logically:*) He just had lunch. If I punched him in the *stomach* he might have *barfed* on me!

Nicki. I mean, why punch him at *all*?!

Doug. Any guy who'd lure a lovely girl like you into a sordid affair—! (*too angry to continue, moves down* s.l.; *she countermoves* s.r.)

Nicki. Douglas, are you crazy?

Doug. (*facing her, BOTH now downstage of sofa*) Do you *deny* you and Jason are driving up to Connecticut for the weekend?

Nicki. Of course not! But didn't you hear us discussing *why* we're going?

Doug. (*turns away, folds arms*) I didn't stick around for the *lurid* part!

Nicki. (*laughs, moves to him*) Oh, Doug, you loveable dope! (*turns him to face her*) If you *had* stuck around, you'd have heard that the *reason* we're going to Connecticut is to get *married*!

Doug. (*gape-jawed*) Married?! But—you *can't* marry Jason!

Nicki. Aw, Doug, I can understand why you're upset, but—oh, I know you and I have had a very pleasant relationship for awhile, but—

Doug. Nicki, you're not paying attention! I didn't say you *mustn't* marry him, I said you *can't*!

Nicki. (*coolly, taking backstep from him into armchair area*) Oh? And why *can't* I?

Doug. Well, for one thing, his *wife* might object!

NICKI. (*flops into armchair*) His *what*?!

DOUG. (*drops to his knees before her, clutches her hands*) Nicki, didn't Jason tell you *anything* about where he works?

NICKI. Murdock and Moran? What's to tell? They make patent medicines. Anyone who needs aspirin, cough syrup, antacids, athlete's foot lotion or a laxative is probably buying it from good old M-and-M! Jason keeps tabs on their profits — which are *sinfully* huge!

DOUG. Nicki, I don't mean his job, I mean the corporate by-laws! You *can't* be a company officer at M&M unless you've got a *wife*!

NICKI. Doug, you're talking nonsense! Jason's already on their Board of Directors!

DOUG. My point exactly! And if he *didn't* have a wife, he'd still be in the *typing* pool!

(*PHONE; they look at it as NAOMI enters K.R. to answer it; she stops as she sees DOUG still on his knees holding NICKI's hands.*)

NAOMI. *Another* proposal of marriage? Remind me to borrow your perfume! (*PHONE; she moves for it again while DOUG hastily regains his feet.*)

NICKI. Honestly, Naomi, why would I marry Doctor Procter?!

NAOMI. Free blood test? (*answers PHONE just as it rings again*) Kingsley residence . . . Oh, *yes*, sir, we've been *wondering* where you —

NICKI. (*rises, moves toward NAOMI, DOUG following a short distance*) Is that Jason?

NAOMI. (*nods to her while continuing on phone:*) Yes, Mister Kingsley . . . About ten minutes? Good, see you then . . . Yes, sir . . . All right. (*hangs up*) Well, we've solved our mystery!

NICKI. Oh, good! Who *is* it?

NAOMI. Thornton Murdock.

NICKI. Jason's *boss*?

DOUG. What *about* him?

NICKI. (*as if it were obvious*) *He* is the third person!

DOUG. What is this, a grammar lesson?

NAOMI. She means our mysterious third person for *dinner*! (*starts toward* K.R.) Mister Kingsley stopped off to buy champagne, that's why he's late getting home. (*exits* K.R. *during:*)

DOUG. Nicki, what's all this about dinner? I thought you and Jason were leaving for Connecticut the moment he got home?

NICKI. So did *I*! But maybe his boss wants to give us his blessing, or something, before we go.

DOUG. Thornton Murdock doesn't give blessings to *bigamists*! Have you forgotten Jason's *wife*?!

NICKI. He hasn't *got* one! He would have *told* me!

DOUG. Not while proposing *marriage*!

NICKI. Doug, what you're saying is nonsense! *You're* a company officer and *you* don't have a wife . . . *do* you?

DOUG. Of course not, I'm just a *medical* officer — "Say *aaah* and bend over!" — I don't make any executive decisions. The only thing *I* run there is a cold *stethoscope*!

NICKI. But — a *wife* doesn't make executive decisions, either!

DOUG. No, but she gives dinner parties for important clients, and she attends social functions on her husband's arm — *and* relays all the gossip from the Ladies Room so her husband knows what his business associates are *really* planning to do!

NICKI. That's *horrible*!

DOUG. (*shrugs*) It's a fact of corporate life! If Jason's on the Board, Jason's married.

NICKI. Oh, Doug! . . . Have—have *you* met—Jason's wife?

DOUG. Well, as a matter of fact—I haven't . . . but those affairs are pretty crowded, it'd be easy to miss her . . . but that rule about married officers is so strict that—

NICKI. Doug! That's *it*! Jason *hasn't* got a wife—he *needs* one! *That's* why he proposed today, so unexpectedly! He must be up for some *big* promotion and—

DOUG. —and *you're* the handiest *steppingstone*?

NICKI. That's a *rotten* thing to say!

DOUG. The truth really hurts, doesn't it!

NICKI. (*icily, pointing doorward*) I think you'd better leave!

DOUG. (*starts that way*) Why not! I hope you'll be very happy—taking notes in the Ladies Room! (*exits to hall, slamming door after him; as NICKI makes incoherent noises of frustration and rage, NAOMI enters K.L.*)

NAOMI. Who came *in*?

NICKI. That was Douglas Procter going *out*—out of this apartment, and out of my *life*!

NAOMI. (*looks keenly at her unhappy face*) What do *you* care, Miss Channing? You're in love with Jason Kingsley, right—?

NICKI. (*startled*) Why—of *course* I am! I mean—why else would I be *marrying* Jason?! (*doesn't want to think about it, heads for* B.R.) Excuse me, I've got to fix my face!

NAOMI. When you're through repairing your *surface* parts, how about a stiff drink?

NICKI. (*off*) Don't be silly, Naomi—and make it a double!

(*As NAOMI goes to sideboard and fixes a scotch on the rocks, JASON KINGSLEY, a personable young man in his mid-20s and a three-piece suit, enters from hall almost at a run, slamming door behind him, and sees NAOMI with drink in her hand as he enters living room.*)

JASON. Mrs. Schuyler! Are *you* what's been happening to my scotch?

NAOMI. Only on long afternoons. This is for Miss Channing.

JASON. She's here?! That's a relief! I wasn't sure, after giving her such short notice! (*absently takes glass from NAOMI, drains it; then:*) Is that her suitcase?

NAOMI. Unless *I'm* eloping with the *gas man*! (*starts fixing second drink in fresh glass*)

JASON. Who's *that* one for?

NAOMI. Miss Channing. The last one didn't do her much good.

JASON. (*looks at empty glass in his hand*) Oh. Sorry about that. (*sets glass on sideboard*) I'm a little nervous today.

NAOMI. (*quick glance toward* B.R., *then, lowering her voice a notch:*) Not half as nervous as *I* am! It's been touch-and-go, the past ten minutes with your unexpected *fiancee* popping up on the premises! You could have *warned* me!

JASON. I forgot. I've been in such a state of terror since Mister Murdock invited himself over here that some of the finer details slipped my mind—such as my engagement! (*absently takes second drink from her, starts sipping at it, as she stoically starts making a third drink, during:*)

NAOMI. You really *should* have told me, you know. When you struck out with Miss *Magruder* this morning, and didn't know where to turn, I decided to see what *I* could do, and —

JASON. (*abruptly terrified*) Miss Magruder?! You didn't mention *her* to Miss Channing, did you?!

NAOMI. What, tell your adoring fiancee that she got proposed to at lunch because *another* girl turned you down at *breakfast*? I didn't have the heart. Miss Channing is *so* much in love — her eyes are sparkling, her feet almost float above the floor — !

JASON. I did *not* propose to Poopsie Magruder! I just asked her to be my wife!

NAOMI. Aren't you splitting hairs?

JASON. For this *evening* I asked her! Just to *pretend* to be my wife till Murdock went away! (*belatedly defensive*) And it wasn't over breakfast! I managed to catch her at the bus stop on her way to work, and explained my predicament till the bus arrived. She said she'd love to help, but on Friday nights she washes her hair. (*finishes drink, sets glass on sideboard*)

NAOMI. Mister Kingsley, that's not the point! The point is, when you phoned this morning in terror and told me Miss Magruder said no, I remembered that my sister's girl is in town this week, and I thought that maybe *she'd* be willing to help — I mean, she *is* in show business — acting the part of your wife should be easy as pie — so —

JASON. Look, there's no time to chat, now. I've got to explain the whole sordid situation to Miss Channing before Murdock gets here!

NAOMI. Stop worrying. Your Nicki has a loving heart

and a good head on her shoulders, and I'm *sure* once you explain matters—

JASON. Who's *Nicki*? Do you mean *Monica*?

NAOMI. As a dental technician, she thinks the shorter version sounds friendlier to those terrified souls in the dentist-chair.

JASON. Nonsense. It doesn't alliterate right for the wife-to-be of a corporate officer. "Nicki Kingsley" sounds much too casual; now, "*Monica* Kingsley" has *class*!

NAOMI. Be that as it may—do me a favor: When you're *not* flaunting her to your fellow boardmembers— in those homier moments when you take her into your arms—call her "Nicki"? A *husband* should sound *friendly.*

JASON. Look, can't we discuss romantic approaches *after* I get back from the honeymoon? Right now, I've got to get that champagne on ice, and—(*realizes*) The champagne! It's on the floor in the apartment lobby! I set it down while I was getting out my door key! (*heads doorward just as NICKI re-enters* B.R.)

NICKI. Darling! . . . Where are you going?

JASON. My champagne's on the floor of the lobby— and there are *winos* out front! (*exits*)

NAOMI. (*hands her the fresh drink*) Here, you'll be needing this!

NICKI. (*taking glass gratefully and taking a quick sip; then:*) Naomi . . . does Jason's mood strike you as—um—strange, somehow? I mean, I know grooms tend to be nervous, but—well—I mean—you'd think he'd give his bride-to-be a big kiss and hug the moment he saw her, regardless. Wouldn't he. . . ?

NAOMI. Mister Kingsley is just . . . highstrung. His

work is very demanding. After all, being treasurer for a billion-dollar corporation—

NICKI. But that's *business*! Right now, *away* from the office—well—you'd think he'd be just a *little* more romantic . . .

NAOMI. (*thinks a second, comes to a decision*) Look . . . Miss Channing . . . these walls aren't very thick. I *heard* you and Doctor Procter talking. I *know* what's making you feel uneasy and uncertain—

NICKI. Naomi! What an idiot I've been! If *anyone* could clear up the mystery of Jason's marital situation, *you* could!

NAOMI. *No* I couldn't! I mean, I *could*, but as a loyal employee I couldn't. Besides, Mister Kingsley made me swear that I'd *never* tell the truth about him to *anyone*! It's *his* secret, after all, and without his permission—! No. *I'll* never tell!

NICKI. Never tell *what*?

NAOMI. (*almost falling into the trap*) That he— (*stops, gives NICKI admiring look*) Tricky little thing, aren't you!

NICKI. It was worth a try.

NAOMI. Look, I've got to see to dinner, our guest will be here any minute. I'm sure Mister Kingsley will be happy to clear matters up for you when he gets back. (*exits K.R.*)

NICKI. I'll drink to *that*! (*as she takes second sip of drink, DOORBELL*)

NAOMI. (*off*) Oh, damn!

NICKI. (*setting glass on sideboard*) Relax, I'll get it! (*goes to door, opens it, JASON lurches in past her with large bag cradled in both arms, moving toward K.L. on:*)

JASON. Thanks, I couldn't reach my key! (*halts as*

NAOMI emerges K.L. *and takes bag from him*) You're a lifesaver, Mrs. Schuyler! Would you get this stuff into the icebucket, fast?

NAOMI. Love to. I may just dive in *after* it! (*exits* K.L. *with bag; as JASON reacts to her line:*)

NICKI. Jason, why *do* you have it so hot in your apartment? I mean, July in New York—!

JASON. (*clasps both her hands in his*) It's a long story, Monica. I'll *try* to tell you everything before T.B. gets here, but if I don't make it, play along with me, okay?

NICKI. Who's T.B.?

JASON. Mister Murdock! Thornton Beresford Murdock! We always call him "T.B."

NICKI. But that's a deadly disease!

JASON. And don't think it doesn't *suit* him! But listen—(*tows her into area just above sofa*)—I've got to fill you in fast, so pay close attention—!

NICKI. Jason, aren't you even going to *kiss* me?

JASON. You mean *now*?!

NICKI. It *is* a customary greeting to one's fiancee . . . (*leans face toward him, puckers up*)

JASON. Later! There are more *important* things to do! Did you pack a nightgown?

NICKI. Of *course* I did!

JASON. Terrific! (*grabs up suitcase, hands it to her, propels her toward* B.R.) Go get into it!

NICKI. Jason! What *is* this? Why aren't we heading for Connecticut to get married? You said—

JASON. Darling, of *course* we'll get married! (*propels her toward* B.R. *again*) But right now I need you in that nightgown!

NICKI. Jason, what do you think I am?! You said the moment you got home, we'd hop in the car—

JASON. And we will, darling, honestly we will! But then this thing with T.B. came up and—

NICKI. Jason, I've already sublet my apartment! If we don't drive to Connecticut, where am I going to *sleep* tonight?

JASON. Why, *here*, of course! Then in the morning we hop in the car and—

NICKI. (*drops suitcase, sad and disillusioned*) Oh, Jason, how could you?! That's not even *original*! I thought you were *above* the old "first-stay-the-night-and-*then*-we'll-get-married" routine! I thought you *loved* me!

JASON. Monica, I *do* love you! And we *are* getting married tomorrow!

NICKI. But only if we make whoopee tonight? Jason, don't you have *any* respect for me at all?

JASON. Monica, I do *not* want to make *love* to you!

NICKI. (*reacts*) *Ever?!*

JASON. (*at wit's end*) Before we're *married*, I mean!

NICKI. Then *why* do you want me to put on that *nightie*?

JASON. 'Cause Mister Murdock expects it!

NICKI. (*horrified*) Jason!

JASON. He's *not* coming here to *violate* you, just to *look* at you!

NICKI. (*takes backstep, arms crisscrossed on her breast*) Jason!

JASON. Damn it, this has *nothing* to do with *sex*! (*storms over to area between coffeetable and sofa, laments out front:*) How could you even *think* such a thing?!

NICKI. (*moving slowly in his direction, trying to piece matters out*) Your boss is coming over to see me in my nightie and I shouldn't think about *sex*?

JASON. (*explodes*) He thinks you have an incurable *disease*!

NICKI. So what's he trying to do, *catch* it?!

JASON. He's coming here to *cure* it!

NICKI. I thought it was *incurable*?!

JASON. (*almost in tears*) Damn it, so did *I*! (*slumps down on sofa*) People were dying of it quite peacefully for years and years, and then some *idiot* has to come up with a *treatment* for it! (*buries his face in his hands*)

NICKI. (*more sympathetic now than upset, moves toward him*) Jason . . . *what* are you talking about? (*He looks up; she gently takes his hand.*)

JASON. Oh, Monica — I'm so ashamed . . .

NICKI. Tell me anyhow.

JASON. (*shrugs, sighs*) All right. Rising young executives at Murdock and Moran have to be married! Were you aware of that?

NICKI. I — well, I've heard *something* about it, yes . . . I thought that's why you and I —

JASON. Monica, you don't understand. I'm *not* a rising young executive — I've already *riz*!

NICKI. Jason, then I don't understand at all! Did they make an *exception* in your case, or — ?

JASON. (*grimly*) There are *no* exceptions at Murdock and Moran!

NICKI. Then how could you possibly — ? Oh!

JASON. Exactly! I told them I *was* married when I first *started* there!

NICKI. (*getting a glimmering, slowly sits beside him during:*) I see . . . yes, I'm beginning to see . . . but — What about social events — company dinners — entertaining at home — ? How could you manage all these years to keep them thinking —

JASON. (*twists to face her, takes both her hands*) My wife is an *invalid*! I mean, if I *had* a wife, she *would* be! It worked perfectly — nobody ever *expected* to see her at company gatherings — and they *certainly* couldn't expect her to do any *entertaining*—not with *LaBeck's* Syndrome!

NICKI. What's LaBeck's Syndrome?

JASON. What she's *got*, of course!

NICKI. I *figured* that much! I mean, what kind of disease *is* it?

JASON. (*stands, paces, eyes alight, as he expounds:*) It was just plain *perfect* for my purposes! No pain, no disfigurement, no big medical bills—after all, how could I have *faced* going in to the office every day if all my co-workers expected a continuing *progress*-report on my wife? No, it's really a rather *nice* disease. That's why I *picked* it!

NICKI. But, what does it *do*? How does it *work*?

JASON. (*stops pacing, leans over her, enthuses:*) It's caused by hyperactive sweat-glands! The symptoms are acute lassitude and chronic syncope!

NICKI. What's that in English?

JASON. The victim's always zonked and *faints* a lot!

NICKI. Sounds something like terminal *consumption*!

JASON. It *is* quite similar—except there's no coughing.

NICKI. Sort of like *Camille* without the *cuspidor*. . . ?

JASON. (*drops down beside her on sofa, anxiously*) *Don't* make jokes!

NICKI. Sorry. I was just trying to get a *handle* on the thing!

NAOMI. (*off*) The situation or the cuspidor?

NICKI. These walls *are* thin, aren't they! Does—does Naomi know about the wife-setup?

JASON. Naturally! How could I have a housekeeper who couldn't answer the phone?

NICKI. The phone?

JASON. People *do* call to see how Lavinia's doing!

NICKI. Whoa! Who's Lavinia?

JASON. (*takes her fondly by the hands*) If you marry me tomorrow—*you* are!

NICKI. (*pulls hands free, recoils*) *What?!*

JASON. Oh, darling, don't desert me now! I swear, right after we get back from Connecticut, we'll have your name changed legally to "Monica"!

NICKI. (*stands, takes backstep from him*) My name *is* "Monica"! Why don't we just *leave* it that way?!

JASON. (*rises, moves toward her as she backs away below armchair*) You don't understand—I've already *told* everyone my wife's name is "Lavinia," so *that* name has to be on the *license*!

NICKI. Jason, are you nuts?! If I marry you as "Lavinia" while my name is "Monica" the marriage won't be *valid*! Even *Connecticut* has *some* principles!

JASON. (*manages to grasp her hands again and stop her retreat*) Look, old man Murdock will *be* here any *minute*! Can't we work out these teensy technicalities *later*?!

NICKI. "Teensy"?! You ask me over here on false pretenses that it's our wedding night, you want me to greet your boss in my nightie, you want me to go through an illegal marriage ceremony tomorrow, and worst of all you expect me to answer to "Lavinia"?! (*with sarcasm he completely misses*) Any *other* little instructions?

JASON. Yes. Whatever you do, don't complain about the *heat*!

NICKI. (*taken totally off base*) Why *not*?!

JASON. Because you *need* it to stay *alive*!

NICKI. *What?!*

JASON. It's because of the way LaBeck's Syndrome *kills* people: The sweat-glands superfunction till the victim succumbs to hypothermia!

NICKI. What's *that* in English?

JASON. You *cool* yourself to death!

NICKI. Jason, then why keep this place like a *steamroom*? Won't it make me sweat even *harder*?

JASON. Not when it's this *humid*, don't you see? The sweat can't *evaporate* to *cool* you, so you have nothing at all to fear!

NICKI. How about death by *drowning*?

JASON. Aw, Monica—!

NICKI. (*relents*) I'm sorry. Really. It's just that what you did is so idiotic—!

JASON. But you'll help me *anyhow*, won't you!

NICKI. But *how*? What do you expect me to—?

JASON. Nothing easier! Just get into that nightie, pretend to be Lavinia when Murdock arrives, and we'll head for Connecticut the moment he goes out that door!

NICKI. *Wait* a minute! It's just occurred to me—why is he coming *through* that door in the *first* place? I mean, so okay, there's now a *cure* for this LaBeck's Syndrome, but what's that got to do with your *boss*? How is *he* supposed to cure me?

JASON. Damned if *I* know! But when he invited himself over, that's what he *said*! The point is—will you *help* me—?

NICKI. (*hesitates; then:*) Oh . . . all right, darling, of *course* I will! (*picks up fallen suitcase, heads toward* B.R.) There must be insanity in *both* our families! (*exits*)

JASON. (*calls after her*) I'll *never forget* you for this, Monica!

NICKI. (*off*) Speaking as your bride-to-be, that's very comforting!

NAOMI. (*enters* K.R., *starts clearing used glasses from sideboard*) I just checked the oven. It's not *quite* as hot as the *kitchen*!

JASON. I'm sorry, Naomi—but if Murdock is up on

his LaBeck's Syndrome info, he's going to *expect* the place to be hot and humid!

NAOMI. (*moving to* K.R. *with glasses*) Don't worry about me; I keep looking on the bright side.

JASON. (*despondent, pours himself a straight scotch with no ice*) *What* bright side?

NAOMI. If this place gets any hotter, I won't have to use the bun-warmer! (*exits; JASON sighs, moves to verge of* B.R.)

JASON. Monica, are you almost ready?

NICKI. (*off*) In a minute, in a minute! Relax! You want me to look my *best* for your boss, don't you?

JASON. Actually—I'm not sure—I wasn't able to find out what a LaBeck's victim *looks* like!

NICKI. (*off*) Then your boss probably doesn't know, either! But I wish you'd given *me* a little more notice, so I could bone up on the *symptoms*!

JASON. There wasn't time! They only *discovered* the cure this *morning*!

NICKI. (*off*) And your *boss* is curing me *tonight*? How could he *possibly*?

JASON. Apparently it's not a *new* medicine. It was just never used on *LaBeck's* before! Seems that somebody with *your* disease took somebody else's medication by mistake, and it *cured* him! No telling *what* happened to the guy who got *his* medication by mistake!

NAOMI. (*off*) They're probably *both* suing the hospital for malpractice. Lotta *money* in that, lately!

(*JASON has moved from* B.R. *nearer* K.R. *as she speaks, so has his back turned to* B.R. *as NICKI enters in a very attractive pair of baby-doll pajamas.*)

NICKI. Well, what do you think?

JASON. (*has just taken sip of drink before turning; turns, sees her, and sprays scotch everywhere as he chokes; then:*) What kind of an outfit is *that*?!

NICKI. (*looks down at herself uncertainly*) What's *wrong* with it?

JASON. (*almost a sob of despair*) I need a *sickie*, not a *centerfold*!

NICKI. (*crushed*) But — I thought this would be my wedding night — and I j-just wanted to look pretty for you — !

JASON. (*contrite at once, sets glass on sideboard and goes to her*) And you *do*, darling, you *do*! But — please — can't you put on a *robe* — ?!

NICKI. (*weepily*) I didn't pack one! Who wears a bathrobe in *July*?

JASON. (*gently ushering her toward* B.R.) Don't fret, darling, *I* have a robe hanging on the door-hook in the bathroom — maybe if you put *that* on over those babydolls you'll look more sickly than sexy!

NICKI. (*brightens at once*) You think I look *sexy*, huh?

JASON. (*takes her in his arms*) So totally torrid and sexy that if I weren't an honorable man, and Murdock wasn't due here any minute, I'd — (*DOORBELL; he shoves her toward* B.R. *instantly.*) Murdock! Quick, darling, get that *robe* on! (*sees her crushed look, softens*) If you love me. . . ? Please. . . ?

NICKI. (*relents, smiles*) Oh, of course I will, darling! Be back in a flash! (*exits* B.R. *as he shouts after her:*)

JASON. But walk *slowly*! (*DOORBELL; he lurches toward foyer, getting to front door just as NAOMI enters via* K.L.) It's okay, Mrs. Schuyler, I've got it! You just relax and play it cool!

NAOMI. In *this* steambath?! (*but exits* K.L. *anyhow, as*

JASON — after taking hold of knob, taking a deep breath, then releasing it and forcing a smile — opens door; it finally is THORNTON MURDOCK; he is tall, flint-eyed, in mid-50s, wears an expensive 3-piece suit, and even when smiling looks rather dangerous; as he steps into foyer:)

JASON. T.B.! Welcome to my humble home at last! *(pumps his hand fervently while kicking door shut gently; over next few lines, they'll make their way to area just before sofa)*

T.B. Thank you, Kingsley.

JASON. You're welcome, sir!

T.B. Nice little place you have here!

JASON. Thank you, sir!

T.B. Not very adequate for entertaining, however, in the corporate manner.

JASON. No, sir. But because of Lavinia's condition, as you know —

T.B. Of course. I quite understand. But now that remission of her affliction is due —

JASON. I'll move to a much larger place as soon as possible! Tomorrow, if you like!

T.B. Good man! *(looks about, curiously)* But where *is* your wife, Kingsley?

JASON. She'll be joining us in a moment, sir. *(They sit on sofa at either end, JASON left, T.B. right.)*

T.B. Good, good . . . Tell me, Kingsley, man to man . . . how *is* she holding up? It's been a long, long siege.

JASON. Marvelously well, thank you. She — uh — she hardly looks to be ill at all! Still seems to be young, vibrant, beautiful — !

NAOMI. *(enters K.R.)* Can I fix you gentlemen a drink?

T.B. *(stands)* Nonsense! I would *think* of making demands on a woman in your condition! *(to JASON,* sotto voce:) "Young," you said?

JASON. (*stands*) Sir, this is Mrs. Schuyler, my housekeeper!

T.B. Well, *that's* a relief! (*sits again*)

JASON. (*to NAOMI*) And we *will* have that drink, thanks!

NAOMI. (*moving to sideboard*) A double?

JASON. (*with forced smile*) You better believe it! (*sits again; NAOMI will fix two scotch-on-the-rocks during:*)

T.B. Kingsley—you're not—um—*concealing* anything from me, I hope?

JASON. (*trying to mask his terror*) Such as *what*, sir?

T.B. I know you're trying to be brave, but the fact that your wife has not yet joined us speaks for itself—she *is* a lot worse than you've been letting on, isn't she!

JASON. (*relieved, feigns brave resignation*) Who knows?! The visual traces of her affliction can be *quite* deceptive, sir. But she keeps assuring me she feels just fine. It helps. Helps a lot.

T.B. What a *noble* creature she must be—when she might with justification think only of herself, her first concern is not to worry *you*!

NAOMI. (*approaching them with drinks*) She's one-of-a-kind, all right! (*as they take drinks from her:*) Never gets to go out, never gets to meet people, never gets to enjoy a cooling breeze—

JASON. (*fearful she's laying it on too thick*) But always cheery as a chipmunk!

T.B. (*stands, raises glass before him; JASON, sensing what's coming, belatedly stands also, raises own glass*) To Lavinia Kingsley—whose bravery, selflessness and courage would melt a heart of stone—may this night bring her the joy she has so long awaited!

NAOMI. Amen!

(*JASON glares, she ignores him. T.B. misses their
byplay entirely, and JASON resignedly joins him in
a long drink. As they drink, NICKI enters via* B.R.,
*stands just inside room; she's in JASON's robe,
now, and it's a brown terrycloth robe with a hood,
and also* much *too large for her, so that its lower
hem reaches the carpet, and with the hood up — as it
now is — her face cannot even be seen, and she
resembles nothing so much as a Franciscan monk;
NAOMI sees her, looks from her to the drinking
men, shakes her head wearily, and exits* K.R.; *a moment later, his glass empty, T.B. turns his head that
way, reacts, and then moves toward her, leaving his
glass on sideboard en route; JASON is just
finishing drink, and doesn't turn his head till:*)

T.B. Oh! Poor Lavinia! This is *much* worse than I'd
imagined! (*takes her hand and says:*) How *is* the poor
woman, Father?!

JASON. (*reacts, rushes to join them [also abandoning
empty glass on sideboard]*) T.B., you've made a tiny little mistake — *this* is *Lavinia*! (*smiling, but talking
through clenched teeth:*) Why not lower that *hood*,
darling?!

NICKI. (*doing so*) Sorry, Jason, I didn't think.

T.B. My dear! How good of you to arise from your
sickbed to meet me at last!

NICKI. (*since he is still holding her hand, pumps it
vigorously*) It's an *honor*, Mister Murdock!

JASON. (*circumnavigates T.B. to get to her, starts
arm-leading her sofaward*) She's *so* brave! Come, darling, you mustn't stay on your feet too long! (*Somehow,
T.B. gets her other arm — BOTH MEN are now gripping
her by an upper arm — and her feet are no longer on the*

floor as they move her below armchair to position at center of just-below-sofa area.) You really should sit down, and not tire yourself this way!

NICKI. (*kicking her still-airborne legs slightly*) I'm *trying* my *best*! (*MEN realize, set her down on her feet; she sits, says to T.B.:*) Jason is *so* thoughtful. (*JASON will sit on her left, T.B. on her right, during:*)

T.B. I can't tell you how pleased I am to be the bearer of such wonderful tidings!

NICKI. *What* wonderful tidings?

T.B. Kingsley, didn't you *tell* her?

JASON. Tell her *what*?

T.B. About the *cure*!

NICKI. Oh, *those* wonderful tidings! Yes, of course he told me! I'm so *excited*!

T.B. (*abruptly grave, takes her hand*) Oh, my dear, do you think that's really *wise*, under the circumstances?

NICKI. *What* circumstances?

T.B. Kingsley, didn't you *tell* her?

JASON. Tell her *what*?

T.B. That a person with LaBeck's Syndrome must *never* get excited! It makes the sweat-glands close up

NICKI. But isn't that all to the *good*? If I don't sweat, I can't *cool* myself to death!

T.B. My dear, your glands don't stop *trying* to sweat if you get excited—they just *close*!

JASON. You don't mean—?!

T.B. (*nods solemnly*) Too long a term of uninter-rupted excitement—and the victim *blows up*!

NICKI. Jason! You never *told* me!

T.B. Kingsley, how *could* you keep such vital information from her?

JASON. (*thinks wildly; then:*) I didn't want to *excite* her! (*While T.B. and NICKI mull this over, facing out front with slightly befuddled expressions, JASON takes T.B.'s glass and stands.*) Would anybody like another drink? *I* sure would! (*heads for bar, will replenish two glasses, fill a third for NICKI*)

NICKI. (*sees T.B. is about to ask JASON dangerous questions, quickly says:*) Mister Murdock, I—

T.B. "Thornton." Please. And may I call you "Lavinia"?

NICKI. (*winces slightly at the name; then steels herself, and:*) I—suppose you may as well . . . Thornton.

T.B. But you were about to ask—?

NICKI. I was just wondering how you—that is, a busy corporate executive like you—seem to know so much about Lavinia's—about *my*—about LaBeck's Syndrome?!

T.B. (*chuckles*) Actually, I knew next-to-nothing about it till they announced it had been *cured*!

NICKI. (*as JASON starts back with trio of drinks*) But that was only this *morning*! My, you must have been boning up all day!

T.B. (*absently accepting drink from JASON, who's behind sofa*) Didn't have to. They covered the whole thing on *Good Morning America*!

JASON. (*deftly slipping into* s.l. *area, so NICKI has to turn and make eye-contact with him as he hands her a drink, and see the pay-attention look in his eyes, while he feeds her vital information:*) That's where Lavinia and *I* saw it, too! What a *wonderful* moment for the two of us!

NICKI. (*gets it, turns smilingly to T.B.*) *I* was just *thrilled*!

JASON. (*as he resumes his seat beside her, cautionarily adds:*) But *not excited*!

(*Each will raise glass individually on:*)

T.B. Well, here's to the future!

JASON. Here's to medical science!

NICKI. And here's to taking the cure! (*ALL drink; then:*)

T.B. Ah, this is a proud day for Murdock and Moran!

NICKI. It is?

T.B. To think of it—one of *our* medications is actually capable of *curing* something! *Johnson and Johnson* are gonna turn *blue*! When I think of the *publicity*—!

JASON. One of *our* medications?

NICKI. *That's* the cure?

T.B. (*his puzzlement tinged with suspicion*) I thought you said you *watched* what they said on *Good Morning America* . . .

NICKI. (*exchanges panicky glance with JASON, then improvises:*) I must have fainted during the good parts.

JASON. (*any old bandwagon in a storm*) Me, too! (*when BOTH stare at him, realizes this is no good; tries:*) I mean, when Lavinia fainted, I was too busy chafing her wrists to hear the full report!

T.B. (*accepts this, relaxes*) *I* see.

NICKI. (*relieved, blurts:*) That's good! (*when T.B. reacts, covers instantly with:*)—of *you*! To *care* so much about *curing* me!

T.B. Ah, but I am doing even *more* than merely *caring* about your being cured, my dear! I fully intend to see that you *are* cured before I leave this apartment!

NICKI. You brought the medicine *with* you?

T.B. Well, hardly! I'd only trust its administration to a qualified doctor!

JASON. But *we* don't make any *prescription* drugs, sir. . . ?

T.B. The F.D.A changed that the moment the cure was announced! *Steemo* can now only be obtained from a pharmacist! We can *triple* the price! Isn't that great?!

JASON. "*Steemo*"? But that's our *back-rub* liniment! I'm not sure if I want a stranger massaging Lavinia.

NICKI. And this is Friday evening, Thornton — my doctor won't be available until Monday morning! We can *hardly* impose upon you to stay here *that* long!

T.B. I've already taken that into consideration, my dear. I said to myself, "Why should she have to *wait*?" After all these years, it just didn't seem fair! And *so*. . . !

JASON/NICKI. (*echoing him amid smiles too sickly to quite conceal dread*) "And so. . . ???"

T.B. I summoned my *own* doctor to come here tonight and administer the cure!

JASON. And he *agreed*?

NICKI. With the *weekend* already here?

T.B. Well, actually, he wasn't at home — but I left my request on his answering-machine!

JASON. Then you can't be sure he'll be here!

T.B. *Oh*, yes I can!

NICKI. (*instinctively knowing the answer, but hoping against hope*) How can you be so *certain* — ?

`T.B. (*modestly shrugging the fact off*) Well, after all, I pay the man's *salary*!

NICKI. You don't mean — your company medical officer?!

JASON. (*sensing — but not comprehending — her dread*) Darling, is there anything *wrong*. . . ?

NICKI. (*springs to her feet*) It's nothing . . . just one of my *fainting*-spells coming on!

JASON. (*springs to his feet*) *What* fainting-spells? . . . *Oh! Those* fainting-spells!

T.B. Then why are you standing *up*, Lavinia?

NICKI. (*trying to move past him*) I was hoping to make it into the *bedroom* before passing out! I'd rather faint lying down!

T.B. (*as BOTH forestall her exit*) *Nonsense! Much* too risky! You'd better lie down right here on the sofa!

NICKI. But—!

JASON. T.B.'s right, darling. The bedroom's *much* too far! (*She tries again to move that way, anyhow, and once again the men have her each-by-one-arm, her feet off the floor.*)

NICKI. Really, I *hate* to be a burden!

T.B. Don't be silly, you're light as a feather! (*They manage to get her lying on the sofa, her head near* S.L. *area. Over their dialogue:*)

NICKI. But I'm spoiling the dinner party! Nobody likes a *sickie* watching them eat!

JASON. The spell may have *passed* by the time dinner's ready, dear!

NAOMI. (*steps in* K.R.; *her hair looks limp and her face flushed, and she is not quite panting from the heat, but close to it, as she announces:*) Soup's on!

NICKI. (*sits up*) There, you see? Dinner's ready and the spell *hasn't* passed! I'd better go to bed!

JASON. (*smiling gently, but his grip on her shoulder steely as he presses her back down into supine position again*) Nonsense, darling! Just take deep breaths and you'll be fine!

NAOMI. Shall I start serving, sir?

JASON. By all means, yes, Mrs. Schuyler!

T.B. (*noticing for first time*) We seem to be short one chair.

NAOMI. (*half-step deskward on:*) Oh, the desk-chair will do just fine—(*stops motion on:*)

T.B. Here, let *me* get it! (*will move to desk, get chair,*

*position it at upstage edge of table, taking enough time
for next six speeches to be completed*)

NAOMI. Thank you, Mister Murdock. I'll get the soup.
(*exits* K.R.)

JASON. (*in fast* sotto voce *to NICKI*) Monica, what's
this *fainting* bit?!

NICKI. (*similarly, sitting up slightly*) Douglas Procter
knows me!

JASON. Oh, *no*!

NICKI. *Oh*, yes!

JASON. (*pulling her hood back up so only her chin can
be seen under it*) Then *don't* let him see your *face*!

NICKI. (*as T.B. starts back toward them*) But he
knows my *voice*!

JASON. (*his back to T.B., not seeing his approach*)
Well, maybe you could come down with laryngitis,
or — (*It suddenly hits him.*) *How* does Douglas Procter
know your voice?

NICKI. (*spots T.B., already in* S.R. *area*) My, have
you moved that chair *already*, Thornton?!

JASON. (*whirls to face T.B., forging a smile*) You
know, sir, I've been thinking — perhaps Lavinia *should*
go lie down in her bed!

T.B. Kingsley, are you crazy? She's got to *fight* the
fainting-spell!

(*NAOMI will enter* K.R. *with tray of soup-already-in-
bowls, spoons, napkins, and whatever other neces-
sities, and set them out at the three places at the
table, during:*)

NICKI. I *do*? Why?

T.B. Kingsley, didn't you *tell* her?

JASON. Tell her *what*?

T.B. That her body temperature *drops* each time she passes out! Too many faints could be fatal!

NICKI. (*improvises instantly*) But not in *my* bed!

T.B./JASON. Why *not*?

NICKI. It has an electric blanket!

JASON. (*admiring her quickwitted thinking*) Good for you!

T.B. (*puzzled*) What?

JASON. (*reacts, improvises desperately to NICKI*) It's *very* good for you!

NICKI. (*catching the ball deftly, to T.B.:*) Keeps me *toasty*-warm *all* night!

NAOMI. (*now through the table-business*) Come and get it! (*starts toward K.R. with empty tray, but stops for:*)

T.B. What *kind* of soup are we having, Mrs. Schuyler?

NAOMI. Vichysoisse.

T.B. (*takes handkerchief from breast pocket, dabs forehead on:*) Marvelous! I could *use* something nice and cold!

NAOMI. Then you'd better eat it fast! (*exits*)

T.B. (*starts toward table, a nervous JASON and NICKI trailing him*) Is it *always* this warm in your apartment, Kingsley?

JASON. Well, what with Lavinia's affliction—

T.B. That's fine for *her*, of course, but—how do *you* stand it?

JASON. (*who's been dying to do so*) I usually get rid of my coat and tie soon as I get home, sir.

T.B. (*propriety wrestles with the heat momentarily*) I wonder—would you mind if *I*—? (*indicates necktie*)

JASON. Not at all, sir!

(*BOTH MEN gratefully divest themselves of suitjackets and ties, which they will hang on the backs of their chairs [by tacit consensus, T.B. has taken* R. *chair and JASON* L. *chair, with NICKI at desk chair] over following dialogue:*)

NICKI. (*to T.B., pleasantly*) Strip right down to your skivvies, if you like!

JASON. (*shocked*) Lavinia!

T.B. (*not at all shocked, but sincerely grateful:*) I'll keep that in mind! (*tie and jacket off, hesitates, still standing, looks a question to JASON; both pause a second, then will remove vests on:*)

T.B./JASON. Oh, why not!

NICKI. (*will push hood back off her head and sit down during:*) I'm really starved! Didn't eat much lunch today—(*gives significant look at JASON, who smiles weakly*)—and my stomach is ready to telegraph the World Hunger Bureau! (*MEN chuckle at this, and—vests finally off—will sit down, during:*)

T.B. I must say, Lavinia, for a woman nearly at death's door, you have a lively sense of humor!

NICKI. (*already grabbing up soup spoon*) Well, you see one door, you've seen them all! (*MEN chuckle again, and just as she gets spoon into mouth, DOOR-BELL; T.B. reacts with delight, JASON and NICKI with dread, she with spoon still in mouth, handle jutting out, and both hands frantically raising hood again to mask everything but her chin—and spoon-handle.*)

T.B. (*rising*) Ah, that will be Doctor Procter! I'll let him in, myself! (*As he heads for foyer, NAOMI emerges via* K.L.)

NAOMI. No, let *me* do it, Mister Murdock!

T.B. Nonsense, Mrs. Schuyler, I don't mind.

NAOMI. But *I* do! The outer hall is air-conditioned. I could use the breeze!

T.B. (*at foyer, now*) Then let's do it together!

NAOMI. *Now* you're talking!

(*They open door, and DOUG steps in, look as we last saw him, but now carrying medical bag.*)

T.B. Doctor! How good of you to come! (*will start ushering him into living room, while NAOMI leans out into the hall momentarily, fans face with one hand quickly and briefly, then reluctantly closes door and exits K.L.; all her business during:*)

DOUG. Well, your message *did* say "Or *else!*"

T.B. Ha-ha! My little *joke*, of course!

DOUG. (*wryly*) I laughed all the way here. (*By now the two men have entered living room, and JASON has moved in their direction to greet the newcomer, while NICKI remains frozen at the table, spoonhandle still jutting from her mouth.*)

JASON. (*with hollow heartiness*) Doug! How good of you to come!

DOUG. (*with an iciness that misses T.B. but puzzles JASON*) Good evening, Kingsley. (*notes NICKI at table*) Is that the patient?

JASON. (*blocks him before he can move that way*) Yes, but listen, you've probably got *plans* for the evening, so why don't you just *leave* the medication and I'll see that Lavinia takes the cure!

DOUG. As a matter of fact, I don't *have* the medication. (*sets bag on extreme L. end of sideboard*)

T.B. What? Why not? In my message, I specifically said—

DOUG. Yes, but you *neglected* to inform me that the

F.D.A had made it a *prescription* drug! And I forgot to put my prescription pad into my medical bag, so I couldn't get any at the drugstore.

JASON. But then — why come here emptyhanded?

DOUG. (*with a slightly nasty smile*) Because I felt certain that *you*, as a loyal officer of M&M, would be *sure* to have a bottle in your medicine cabinet!

T.B. Of course he has! . . . Go get it, Kingsley!

JASON. (*whom we — and NICKI and DOUG — can easily see* hasn't *got any*) Sir, I'd love to, except that — uh — well — you see — ?!

NICKI. (*takes spoon out of mouth, comes to her feet, and announces — in a thick Swedish accent that would make Greta Garbo feel right at home:*) He yoost it all on me!

JASON. (*so relieved, he doesn't immediately note the accent, though T.B. does*) Of course! After all, *no* one can cool to death wearing *Steemo*!

T.B. Excuse me, Lavinia, but — did I detect an *accent* just now — ?

NICKI. (*nods vigorously beneath hood*) Ya, you betcha!

JASON. (*almost deranged with fear, improvises*) It's the vichysoisse! Whenever she eats it, it reminds her of her roots! Some sort of side-effect from her affliction!

T.B. But *vichysoisse* isn't Swedish — it's French. . . !?

JASON. She was always weak in geography!

NAOMI. Ya, you betcha!

T.B. Wait, I just thought of something! Maybe all the *pharmacists* in town have tied up the supplies of Steemo, but what about places that *don't* have pharmacies? After all, it's available in all the *supermarkets* — ?! If the F.D.A. hasn't *contacted* them yet — ?

JASON. T.B., that's a brilliant idea!

T.B. Of course it is! (*as NAOMI enters via* K.R. *with three salads on a tray*) Mrs. Schuyler, would you mind running a small errand for me?

NAOMI. (*instantly sets tray on sideboard*) For the chance to get out of this sweatbox, I'd be happy to hand-deliver you a *piano*! (*starts removing apron*)

T.B. Marvelous! Then would you hurry to the supermarket and get us a bottle of Steemo?

NAOMI. "Steemo"? In *this* kind of weather? *Nobody* needs liniment in *July*! (*sees a despairing JASON covering his face with his hands, adds quickly:*) But I'll be *happy* to go, of course!

T.B. (*taking bill from pocket*) Good girl! Here's five dollars, that should cover the cost.

NAOMI. (*moving doorward*) If it doesn't, I'll be sure to mention it to you. (*She will exit to hall, during:*)

JASON. Really, though, Doug, I don't feel right tying up your evening this way. Believe me, I'll be *happy* to handle the matter myself when Mrs. Schuyler returns.

DOUG. (*a bit less icily*) That's—that's kind of you. But I'm afraid it *has* to be administered by a physician.

T.B. It'll *only* be a few minutes from now, Kingsley. That's *hardly* taking a big bite out of Procter's evening.

JASON. (*thinks desperately; then:*) All right. You may as well know the truth: I'm insanely *jealous* of Lavinia! I hate to be bullheaded about this, Doug, but I simply *cannot* allow you to *lay* your *hands* on her!

DOUG. (*stiffly*) This will *not* be a *faith*-healing!

T.B. Oh, but surely, Procter, in a case such as this— with her husband so protective—

JASON. —and Lavinia almost pathologically shy—

NICKI. (*averts gaze, takes super-demure stance*) Ay have nav-ver show my bod-dy to awther man!

DOUG. Perhaps I didn't make the circumstances clear

enough. It would be *illegal* for Jason to administer this medication to his wife; the law is very plain about that!

T.B. Nonsense! *Anyone* can take prescription drugs without being a licensed physician!

Doug. But only a qualified doctor or nurse can give a patient a medical *inoculation*!

(*As JASON and NICKI stiffen with horror:*)

T.B. Ah, *now* I understand! Well, then, that makes all the difference, *doesn't* it, Kingsley!

JASON. (*almost incoherent*) Let me get this straight— do you mean that when Mrs. Schuyler gets back here—

NICKI. (*managing to maintin her accent despite her terrified delivery:*) You're going to shoot me full of Shteemo?!

Doug. Well, that *is* the prescribed method of administration, yes.

JASON. Wait a minute! How *can* it be? When they discovered this stuff could cure LaBeck's Syndrome, didn't they discover it by *accident*?

Doug. That's my understanding, yes.

T.B. (*just as fascinated as JASON*) But what was *liniment* doing in a *hypodermic* needle?

Doug. A new nurse picked up the wrong bottle, or something. Apparently the patient's doctor had recommended that the person be *rubbed* with the stuff, which—(*to JASON and NICKI*) as you both obviously know—has a salutary effect on repressing the symptoms, but the nurse's eyes skipped a line on the chart, or something, and he had this *other* patient due for an antibiotic shot, and—(*shrugs*)—the rest is medical history.

JASON. But—I mean—*liniment* being *injected* into a person? Doesn't that kind of—um—*smart*?

DOUG. (*enthusing, as doctors do*) Not *half* so much as the *needle*! That'd be *my* guess! I mean, shots into a muscle or a vein are painful *enough*, but to get a two-inch needle right into the *armpit*—!

NICKI. (*sways, back of one hand to her [unseen] forehead, says sincerely:*) Ay tank ay going to faint! (*JASON and T.B. both rush for her, each catching an arm.*)

DOUG. That's typical of a LaBeck's victim, of course. You'd better get her into her bed. That way, she can be perfectly relaxed when I give her that shot!

NICKI. Ay doubt that ver-ry motch!

T.B. (*surprisingly, sweeps her up into his arms*) Here, Kingsley, let *me* handle this! (*starts to carry her toward* B.R. *before JASON can protest*)

DOUG. (*looking around room*) Let's see, now—that sofa is long enough for a full-grown adult to lie on—and I suppose there's room for two more people in the bedroom—what am I saying, if you and your wife both sleep there, there's *bound* to be—

T.B. (*just short of exit, stops, puzzled, turns around*) Procter, what *are* you babbling about?

DOUG. Well, immediately following the injection, the patient should be kept flat on the back for at *least* two hours, until the medication can do its work—

NICKI. (*barely masking her terror*) Vait a minute, ay change my mind, ay tink ay keep the syndrome!

T.B. That vichysoisse accent persists a long time, doesn't it!

JASON. Lavinia has *very* deep roots!

T.B. (*to NICKI*) But honestly, my dear, you're becoming trepidatious over nothing! Even if the shot *does* feel uncomfortable for awhile, think of the years of healthy bliss ahead of you!

Doug. Ahead of *all* of you!

Nicki/Men. Vhat?/What? (*The Truth is suddenly dawning on them as ALL wheel slowly to face DOUG.*)

Doug. I thought you knew: LaBeck's Syndrome is highly *contagious*!

Jason. You don't mean—?!

Doug. You've *all* got to have the inoculation.

Jason. (*horrified*) Nonsense! *We* don't have any of the *symptoms*!

T.B. (*starts to sway, imperiling still-carried NICKI, who clings to him, hard*) I think I'm going to faint!

Jason. (*knots fists, stamps foot and reaction-rages at T.B.:*) Blabbermouth! (*and as T.B. reacts and stares at JASON unhappily, and NICKI pulls the hood even farther down over her face, and JASON slumps in despair—*)

THE CURTAIN FALLS

End of Act One

ACT TWO

Curtain rises on same tableau that ended Act One, and we pick up right where we left off:

T.B. Kingsley! Did *you* just call *me* a *blabbermouth*?

JASON. (*recovering a smidgin of sanity*) *You*, sir? *Never*, sir! I was talking to *Doug*! (*turns to DOUG instantly*) What kind of doctor *are* you, blabbing all those horrible details in front of an *invalid*?!

DOUG. (*logically*) But I *always* forewarn my patients about reactions to medication! That way, when all the *discomfort* sets in, they don't think something's *wrong*!

T.B. You call a two-inch needleful of liniment in the armpit *discomfort*?! What do you call a broken leg — the *Pleasure Principle*?! (*absently hands NICKI to JASON, moves toward* B.R. *on:*) I've got to lie down!

JASON. (*still holding NICKI, half-turns* B.R., *and overlap of lower robe falls away from NICKI's legs as he says:*) But sir —

DOUG. (*reacts to sight of legs, points at them and shouts:*) Nicki!

T.B. (*stops short of exit, turns*) *What* did you say?

NICKI. (*extemporizing desperately, still Swedish*) Ay have a lousy razor!

JASON. (*picking up the ball*) So when she shaves her legs —

DOUG. (*catching the ball*) — they get all *nicky*!

T.B. (*leans over legs, peers closely at them*) They look all right to *me*. . . ?

JASON. (*gazing at them admiringly*) You can say *that* again!

DOUG. (*similarly*) Yessiree!

NICKI. (*demurely re-covering legs*) Tank you very motch!

T.B. (*to DOUG*) Then why did you shout they looked *nicky*?

JASON. (*getting a new ball into play*) *Not* to the *average* eye, of course!

DOUG. (*fielding the ball*) But to the eye of a trained *physician*, well—!

NICKI. (*face still invisible beneath hood, of course*)—it's plain as the nose on my face!

T.B. (*looks vainly toward where her face should be, shakes head in a real daze, totters once more toward* B.R. *on:*) I've got to lie down!

JASON. (*the instant T.B. exits, sets NICKI on her feet, BOTH rush to DOUG*) Oh, golly, Doug, you were great!

NICKI. *Thanks* for not giving the game away!

DOUG. Okay-okay, but what the hell *is* the game? Nicki, why are you here dressed like that? Why does old man Murdock think you're Lavinia Kingsley?

NICKI. It's very simple, Doug. Jason *doesn't* have a wife! But now that there's a *cure* for his imaginary wife's disease, he's got to *get* a wife fast, or he'll lose his job!

DOUG. Nicki, you can't marry a man just to keep him gainfully employed!

JASON. I resent that! She happens to be in *love* with me!

DOUG. And you with her?

NICKI. Doug, what a thing to ask! (*to JASON*) But answer him anyway, just to *show* him!

JASON. Of *course* I love her! And what business is it of yours in the first place?!

NICKI. Jason—I should have told you—Doug and I used to *date* a little. Just a *little*, though. We hardly saw much of each other at all.

JASON. Is that why it took him so long to recognize your *legs*?!

NICKI. (*pleased*) Why, Jason! You're jealous! How nice of you. That's very flattering.

JASON. Aw, Monica, I should have married you the day we first met! I should have proposed the moment you took your hand out of my mouth!

DOUG. How's that again?

NICKI. Doug, you *know* I'm a dental technician!

DOUG. Oh. Well, yes, but—I just didn't realize you two'd met during business hours.

JASON. Never mind all that! The thing is, what do we all do *now*?!

NICKI. Well, we *don't* get that needle in the *armpit*, at least!

JASON. But T.B. will get suspicious if we don't!

DOUG. No problem. When he comes out, I'll just tell him I already *gave* you the shots!

NICKI. But what about his *own* shot?

JASON. Yeah, he's *sure* to wonder if you don't do the same for him!

NICKI. Oh, but you couldn't subject the poor man to all that unnecessary discomfort! *Could* you?

DOUG. Of course not! I'll just trump up some tale about him having natural immunity, or—well, I'll think of something. Shouldn't be too hard to convince him.

JASON. Not when he considers the *alternative*! Brrr! I *hate* needles!

NICKI. Oh! I just realized—Doug can't tell Thornton we've had our shots if Naomi hasn't come back yet with the Steemo! (*DOORBELL*)

JASON. Saved by the bell! She must've gone out without her key! (*starts doorward*) I'll fill her in on the plot-adjustments fast!

NICKI. Well, *I'm* getting something to eat! (*starts for kitchen via* K.R.) That soup's at *room* temperature by now, and my stomach's starting to sound like a bad *cello*-player!

JASON. There are some crackers and stuff in the pantry!

DOUG. Sounds great to *me*! I haven't had dinner, and I was too upset to eat lunch! (*DOUG and NICKI will exit* K.R. *and JASON reaches hall door, on:*)

NICKI. Well, we can fix that, all right!

(*They've no sooner vanished than JASON has the door open, and POOPSIE MAGRUDER steps in; she is a lovely young lady of about 20 years of age and a cheery outgoing manner and an echo chamber where she should have a brain; she smiles radiantly at JASON as she steps into foyer, on:*)

POOPSIE. Hiiii!

JASON. (*horrified*) Poopsie! What are *you* doing here?!

POOPSIE. Well, I got to thinking, on the bus — you're really not such a bad guy, and you're in a rough spot with this Lavinia-thing and all, and my hair wasn't *that* dirty, so — I've come to play your wife!

JASON. (*as T.B., after a furtive peek through* B.R., *tiptoes into dining area*) Oh, damn! Look, Poopsie, you're really a doll coming through for me this way, but — (*stops in horror as he hears:*)

T.B. (*keeping voice low*) Psst! Kingsley! Where are you?

JASON. (*similarly*) Poopsie, stay right where you are and don't move! (*dashes into living room, rushes toward T.B., whom he will press backwards toward* B.R., *during:*) T.B.! How nice to see you again! Something I can do for you, especially in the other room?!

T.B. Yes! Help me find the fire escape! (*tries to tug JASON off via* B.R., *but JASON resists moving*)

JASON. We're only on the third floor. I'm sure the hook-and-ladder will reach.

T.B. Stop talking like you're humoring a lunatic! *I* know there's no fire! All I want to do is get away from Doctor Procter till I can get a second opinion!

JASON. What you need is a tranquilizer. I've got a bottle in the bathroom cabinet.

T.B. (*takes step toward* B.R., *stops, turns head*) *Our* brand?

JASON. Does it really matter?

T.B. (*shakes head sadly*) Not any more. *Nothing* matters any more! (*abruptly swivels and—not quite half-mad with fear, but probably about one-third—clutches JASON's shirtfront, crouching against him, peering in all directions like a man pursued by demons as he babbles:*) I can't help it. I hate needles. Hate pain. Always have. Always will. And I'm trapped in here with a mad doctor and a hypo full of liniment! Help me! You've *got* to help me! I'll do anything. I'll give you money. *Lots* of money.

JASON. (*has been trying to get a word in throughout this near-incoherent tirade, finally claps his hand gently over T.B.'s mouth, so he can say:*) You're overwrought. Come with me. Trust me. Everything is going to be all right. (*leads him off* B.R.; *even as they vanish, a curious POOPSIE belatedly steps into living room but stops motion as DOUG and NICKI enter* K.R.)

DOUG. Could have *sworn* I heard Mister Murdock out here—?!

NICKI. And where in the world has *Jason—*? (*stops as she sees POOPSIE; DOUG abruptly turns her way, too, on:*)

POOPSIE. Hi! Are you Mister Murdock? I'm Lavinia Kingsley!

NICKI. (*shocked and disillusioned*) You *can't* be!

Jason doesn't *have* a wife!

POOPSIE. Silly, he *has* to have a wife to work at Murdock and Moran! Everybody knows that!

NICKI. (*furiously tearing off robe, starting for front door*) But the *fiancee* is *always* the last to know! (*pauses long enough to fling robe over POOPSIE's arm*) Make that "*former* fiancee"! (*will storm proudly to foyer and exit to hall, during:*)

DOUG. (*starting gallantly after her*) I've got to stop her! She can't *possibly* be carrying *busfare*! (*just short of exit, stops and turns for:*) Where have you *been* till now, anyhow?

POOPSIE. I just got off work.

DOUG. "Work"? But you're an *invalid*!

POOPSIE. Well, *yes*, but I'm not a *fanatic* about it! (*As DOUG reacts in speechless confusion, she holds up robe.*) What should I do with *this*?

DOUG. Considering your medical condition, you'd better put it *on*! (*when she looks at it hesitantly:*) Trust me, I'm a doctor!

(*DOUG exits to hall, closing door after him; after a puzzled look toward where he's just vanished, POOPSIE shrugs and dons robe, putting hood up; she is just securing its cincture when JASON enters* B.R.; *rushes to her and grabs her in his arms.*)

JASON. Oh, darling, I didn't know *anyone* could be so understanding as *you've* been tonight! I promise you, the instant Mister Murdock goes out that door, you and I will *zoom* up to Connecticut and get married!

POOPSIE. But what will *Alvin* say?

JASON. Who's *Alvin*?

POOPSIE. My new boy friend. He's very possessive.

JASON. Darling, why does your *voice* sound so funny? (*DOORBELL; he immediately releases her and rushes for foyer.*) Oh, good, that's Mrs. Schuyler with the liniment!

POOPSIE. Why are you acting so urgent about *liniment* arriving?

JASON. Because we can't get Murdock *out* of here till he's convinced we've injected it into our *armpits!*

(*Even as she reacts — and it's all bafflement, no terror — he has the front door open and NAOMI lurches in with a small paper bag.*)

NAOMI. Wow, this place feels like a blast-furnace! Where do you want the Steemo?

JASON. (*closing door and heading back toward POOPSIE*) Pour about half of it down the sink, then bring the bottle out here and put it on the table!

NAOMI. (*as she exits K.L. with her purchase*) Why didn't you just have me buy the *smaller* size?!

JASON. (*back with POOPSIE, grips her by upper arms*) Now, remember, darling, when Murdock comes back out here, we tell him that *we've* both already *had* our injections!

POOPSIE. *Why?*

JASON. (*impatiently*) So we won't have to *really* get them, of course! Honestly, darling, sometimes you sound as slow on the uptake as — (*is lifting front edge of hood to see her face, and sees it as he says:*) — *Poopsie!*

T.B. (*pops in instantly via B.R., stops just inside room*) *Who* just shouted "Poopsie"?

JASON. *I* did, sir. . . ?

T.B. (*looking left and right in puzzlement*) But who did you shout it *to*?

JASON. (*desperately embraces POOPSIE, one hand on the back of her head to keep it pressed against his chest, her face pointed upstage, as he takes a backstep or two toward* K.R. *area, during:*) To my *wife*, of course! It's a pet name! You know how it is when two people are romantically involved, they always call each other by pet names!

NAOMI. (*entering* K.R. *with half-empty liniment bottle, looks at face of woman JASON is holding, goes stockstill, and blurts:*) Poopsie!

T.B. (*trying not to lose what's left of his mind*) *She* calls your wife "Poopsie," *too*?!

JASON. (*with genius born of desperation, rushes to him, grips his upper arms firmly, and improvises, while NAOMI swiftly guides POOPSIE off via* K.R.) No, sir. She doesn't.

T.B. But I just *heard*—?!

JASON. (*speaking calmly, steadily*) No, sir. You didn't.

T.B. (*fearfully*) Kingsley—what are you trying to tell me—?

JASON. Mister Murdock, I didn't *want* to let you know—I've been hoping on hope that Doctor Procter was wrong—that you *hadn't* been trapped by the contagion—

T.B. (*a terrified near-whisper*) Didn't want to let me know *what*?

JASON. The *side*-effect of LaBeck's Syndrome. It makes you hallucinate!

T.B. Oh, no! Not that! You must be mistaken, Kingsley! They didn't say a *thing* about it on *Good Morning America.* . . ?!

JASON. But just consider, sir — all those sweat-glands starting to superproduce — your body valiantly fighting the invasion, trying *not* to overperspire — all that extraneous perspiration going round and round in the bloodstream, trying to find a place to stop, a place to rest, a place to store up — !

T.B. You — you don't mean — ? (*raising a shaky finger to tap at his temple:*) It all backs up in — *here*?

JASON. (*nods solemnly, pats T.B. consolingly on the shoulder*) What *else* can it do?

T.B. (*fingertips to temples, totters toward sofa*) This is a nightmare! Why can't I wake up! First needles — now madness! (*will sit in center of sofa, a man besieged by fear, during:*) For all I know, I'm not even sitting here on this sofa!

JASON. (*contrite*) I'm *sure* it will all go away soon, sir. Give the tranquilizer a chance to work. You can't expect results in only five minutes. Lie back. Try to relax.

T.B. How can I relax when at any moment Procter's going to — (*half-rises, looks around*) Say, where *is* Procter, anyhow?

JASON. (*realizing absence for first time, also looks around*) Maybe he went into the kitchen. . . ? (*starts for K.R.*)

T.B. (*dashes madly downstage of dining table to chair with his coat, tie and vest, grabbing them up in one hand on:*) Marvelous! Now if you just *keep* him there — ! (*runs upstage of table toward foyer, smiling maniacally*) Now's my chance for that second opinion! Or third opinion! Or whatever it takes!

JASON. (*as T.B. reaches door*) But sir, you've barely touched your dinner . . .

T.B. Mail me a doggy-bag! (*exits to hall, slamming door after him*)

POOPSIE. (*entering via* K.R. *immediately*) Naomi says you already *have* a wife, Jason. . . ?!

JASON. Well—yes and no. It's too confusing to explain right now. Where *is* she, by the way?

POOPSIE. Where is *who*?

JASON. The girl who was wearing that robe!

POOPSIE. Oh, her. She left.

JASON. She *couldn't* have left! Her clothes are still in my bedroom!

POOPSIE. Oh, Jason, *shame* on you!

JASON. It's not what you think! (*starts for foyer*) I've got to find her, she'll get arrested in that outfit!

POOPSIE. I think the doctor was going to give her busfare.

JASON. (*stops on brink of exit to hall*) *He's* gone, *too*? When did all *this* come about?

POOPSIE. Right after I introduced myself. She got all shout-y and took the robe off, and he got all dizzy-looking and made me put it on.

JASON. Why should Doug do a thing like that?

POOPSIE. Who's Doug?

JASON. Douglas Procter, the doctor who told you to put the robe on. Why would he?

POOPSIE. He said because of my medical condition.

JASON. But how could Doug possibly know *your* medical condition—? (*A horrible suspicion occurs.*) Just—what medical condition are we talking about?

POOPSIE. LaBeck's Syndrome. The reason it's so hot in here.

JASON. *You've* got it, *too*?! . . . Oh, no, wait a minute, you *didn't* tell them that you—?! (*smacks palm on forehead*) What am I saying! Of *course* you did! No *wonder* Monica got all shout-y!

POOPSIE. Who's Monica? (*NAOMI re-enters via* K.R.,

*again heading tableward to put that half-empty liniment
bottle there.*)

JASON. Mrs. Schuyler, would *you* explain matters to
Poopsie while I try to find Monica?

NAOMI. (*sets bottle on table*) You mean about
tonight, or just life in general?

JASON. Whatever! (*yanks open door, but before he
can exit, he's nearly bowled over by T.B. rushing in, his
face a mask of terror*)

T.B. He's coming up the stairs! With your *wife* in his
arms! In baby-doll pajamas!

NAOMI. His or hers?

T.B. (*looks that way, reacts to still-hooded POOP-
SIE*) Kingsley! *There's* your wife! But she's also on the
stairs! (*jams heels of hands to temples*) I must be going
bananas!

NAOMI. (*swiftly ushering POOPSIE off via* K.R.)
Here, maybe *this* will help! (*DOORBELL; T.B. gapes,
clutching at JASON.*)

T.B. It's Procter! He mustn't find me! Don't let him!
Please! (*opens coat closet, ducks inside, shuts door;
DOORBELL*)

JASON. (*sighs, opens door; DOUG enters carrying
NICKI*) They wouldn't let her on the bus?

DOUG. *I* wouldn't!

NICKI. Douglas Procter, you put me down this instant!

DOUG. (*setting her on her feet*) I was only trying to
protect your feet from Manhattan sidewalks! It's hard
to propose to a girl with *chewing-gum* between her toes!

JASON. Propose?! To my fiancee?!

NICKI. (*in living room, now, stalking toward* B.R.)
Former fiancee! Or didn't your *wife* remember to *give*
you my message?!

JASON. (*has been striding after her, now stops to wail:*) I don't *have* a wife!

DOUG. (*has moved into living room*) Doesn't surprise *me*! Your Machiavellian attitude toward unsuspecting women —

NICKI. Don't call *me* "unsuspecting"! I've never been so suspicious in my life! (*storms off* B.R., *JASON starts after her again on:*)

JASON. Monica — !

DOUG. (*grabs his arm and stops him*) She's changing her clothes! Don't you have any decency at all?!

JASON. (*tugs free*) Not where *Monica* is concerned! . . . No, wait, let me re-phrase that —

NICKI. (*off*) I thought you phrased it *perfectly*, you louse!

JASON. (*starts toward* B.R. *again*) Monica, I've got to talk to you — I've got to explain why — (*stops as DOUG grabs his arm again*)

DOUG. Do your explaining out *here*, if you don't mind!

NAOMI. (*rushes in via* K.R., *heading for phone, which she will pick up and start dialing furiously; all this during:*) My niece! I forgot all about my niece!

DOUG. (*as both men are distracted from their purpose by her anxiety*) What *about* her niece?

JASON. Search *me*! . . . No, wait, she *did* say something earlier, but I forget what she —

POOPSIE. (*entering* K.R., *hood now thrown back from her head*) Jason, look, as long as your boss isn't here any more, do I have to keep on with —

DOUG. Murdock's gone? How? He didn't pass me on the stairs?!

NAOMI. (*distracts JASON before he can reply, getting her party on phone:*) Hello? . . . This is Mrs.

Schuyler — I phoned earlier with a message for my niece, and — *damn*! (*when TRIO looks her way, explains:*) They put me on hold. I don't mind the waiting, but I hate listening to a rock band playing *Amazing Grace*. . . !

DOUG. (*gets his mind back on track, starts for foyer*) I'd better go look for Murdock. In his panicky mental condition he could stagger in front of a truck!

JASON. (*grabs DOUG's arm*) In his present location, I doubt that very much! He's in my coat-closet!

DOUG. Doing what?

JASON. Hiding from you and your two-inch needleful of Steemo!

POOPSIE. (*with a little shiver*) And who could *blame* him!

DOUG. (*tugs free of JASON's grip, but no longer moves toward foyer*) What are we going to *do*? We can't leave him in there *forever*!

JASON. (*shrugs*) Why *not*? It solves *everything*!

NAOMI. (*dryly*) Sure. We can nail the door shut, and wallpaper over it, and —

NICKI. (*enters* B.R., *now dressed as we first saw her, carrying her suitcase*) Douglas, would you be kind enough to take me to a hotel?

DOUG. (*a bit staggered by this request*) And *then* what?

NICKI. (*exasperated*) Don't be an idiot! It's just that I've sublet my apartment, and —

JASON. Monica, you're not *leaving*?!

NICKI. (*to DOUG*) Catches on quick, doesn't he! (*to POOPSIE*) I hope you two will be *very* happy together!

POOPSIE. But what will *Alvin* say?

DOUG. Who's Alvin?

JASON. Her new *boy* friend!

NICKI. (*uncertainly*) Your wife has a boy friend?!

JASON. She's *not* my wife! She's never *been* my wife! I never *asked* her to be my wife!

POOPSIE. Why, *sure* you did, Jason—I'd just had my breakfast, and started for the bus—

DOUG. When was *this*?

POOPSIE. This morning, of course.

NICKI. (*furiously*) Jason Kingsley! Do you mean to say you proposed to this woman at breakfast, and then proposed to me at lunch?! (*starts past him toward foyer*) Who's gonna be the Lucky Girl at *dinner*!?

NAOMI. (*still standing impatiently with telephone to ear*) My *niece*, if I can't stop her in time!

NICKI. (*stops*) *What?!* (*then, to JASON:*) What kind of Bluebeard *are* you?!

POOPSIE. Jason's in the Campfire Girls?!

JASON. Blue *beard*, not *bird*! (*grabs NICKI, forces her to listen*) Please! If you love me! Pay attention for *just* one minute!

NICKI. (*almost pulls free, then relents, but icily*) All right! But make it good!

JASON. Okay. All I asked Poopsie this morning was to *play* my wife tonight, till T.B. came and departed.

POOPSIE. But I had to wash my hair.

JASON. Poopsie, *please*!

POOPSIE. Sorry.

JASON. (*to NICKI again*) But then I got to thinking—I was in love with you—and hoped you were in love with me—and all these years of *pretending* to be married were a ghastly strain, and—well—I decided it was about time I *really* got married—and you were—have always been—and always *will* be—the *only* girl I want as my wife! So, when I proposed to you at lunch—that was the first time I ever proposed to a woman in my entire life—and that's God's Truth, darling!

NICKI. (*wavering*) Oh, Jason—how I'd like to believe that—but—how do I know you're not just saying it so you won't lose your job?!

JASON. To *hell* with the stupid job! If it's a tossup between marrying you and continuing to work for Thornton Murdock—!

DOUG. Murdock! (*starts for foyer*) He must be *crazed* with fear to stay in that closet all this time! I've got to get him out and *explain* things to him!

JASON. (*releases NICKI, whirls and grabs DOUG*) Doug! You *can't* explain things to him! It would ruin everything!

DOUG. (*yanks free*) Listen, Kingsley, enough is enough! Since when do I owe *you* any favors?! You've just said marrying Nicki—the only woman *I* ever loved—meant more to you than your job with Murdock and Moran; well, *I'm* gonna give you the chance to *prove* it!

NICKI. Oh, Doug, you *can't*!

DOUG. Oh, no? Just *watch* me! (*starts for foyer again*) When I tell Murdock how he's been *deceived* by Jason—!

NAOMI. (*annoyed, hangs up phone as she says:*) And by his own doctor—!

DOUG. (*stops, apprehensive*) What—?

NAOMI. (*smiling "sweetly"*) *Who* told him LaBeck's Syndrome was contagious? *Who* pretended *not* to know Jason was unmarried? And *who* told him he was due for a two-inch needle in the armpit?!

POOPSIE. (*brightly*) Gee, *I* give up, *who*? (*OTHERS look at her incredulously for one fractional moment, then shake their heads and get back on the track with:*)

DOUG. But all of those things can be explained—!

JASON. If he lets you *live* that long.

DOUG. (*stymied, just stands there*) Damn.

NICKI. Oh, but Jason, we've *got* to get Thornton out of that closet *some*time!

NAOMI. If you'll pardon my interfering—

JASON. (*shrugs*) I always *have* . . .

NICKI. Naomi, you've got a *plan*?

NAOMI. Well, nothing that will absolutely *guarantee* success, but—

JASON. Listen, right now I'd even take suggestions from *Poopsie*!

POOPSIE. (*slight frown*) Was that a *crack*?!

JASON. No, just a *fact*!

POOPSIE. (*brightens*) Well, that's *different*, of course! (*Once again, OTHERS look incredulously at her, then get on-track again.*)

DOUG. What *is* your plan, Mrs. Schuyler?

NAOMI. Well, it all hinges on just *how* whacked-out Mister Murdock is—if he believes the part about hallucinating, and his *time*-sense is a bit bent out of shape—

DOUG. Hold on—"hallucinating"? *I* never said—

JASON. No, *I* did! I thought it might smooth over some of the rough spots.

NICKI. But what's his *time*-sense got to do with the situation, Naomi?

NAOMI. Well, when he went off into the bedroom the first time he felt faint, you and Mister Kingsley were supposedly about to get your *liniment*-injections. If we can convince him that *two hours* have gone by since then—

DOUG. Why two hours?

NAOMI. 'Cause *that's* how long *you* said they'd have to *lie down* after their shots!

DOUG. Oh, yeah, I forgot!

JASON. Fine doctor *you* are!

DOUG. Now, listen here—!

NICKI. *Later*, Doug, fight with Jason *later*! Right now, let's listen to Naomi's plan!

DOUG. I'm not sure I *want* to listen!

POOPSIE. Then how will you know what it *is*?

DOUG. (*exasperated*) What I *mean* is, no matter *what* the plan turns out to be, I'm going to end up helping another man get married to the girl I love!

POOPSIE. (*dreamily*) Gee, just like Humphrey Bogart in *Casablanca*!

DOUG. (*not unpleased by the comparison*) Gee, it *is* kinda like that, *isn't* it! (*abruptly frowns*) No, it's not the same at *all*! Ilsa was *already* married to Victor Lazslo! If she was still *single*, Rick would *never* have let her get on that plane!

NICKI. Oh, *sure* he would, Doug! Victor needed her in his *work*, she was the thing that kept him *going—*!

NAOMI. (*who's been trying to get a word in since her last line*) You're *all* going to be on the next plane to Lisbon if you don't stop gabbing and *listen* to me!

JASON. Sorry.

DOUG. (*with wistful enthusiasm*) What's the plan?

NAOMI. (*to JASON and NICKI*) *You* two confront him, all bright-eyed and bushy-tailed, and tell him the cure *worked,* and you're feeling just *fine*! And be *sure* to tell him you didn't feel a *thing* when you got your liniment-hypos! And then *you—*(*to DOUG*)—get your little needle out and *pretend* to give him *his* shot, and everything's *rosy* again!

POOPSIE. And what do *I* do?

JASON. *You* go home and wash your hair!

NICKI. But *after* Thornton gets his shot!

DOUG. Why not before?

NICKI. Because it will take at *least* four people to hold him down while you *give* him the shot!

POOPSIE. Including *me*?

JASON. (*looks at her, almost speaks, then shakes his head, and:*) Doug, *will* you help? All you have to do is *swab* him with something to supposedly dull the pain, then get out your needle and pretend to inject him with the Steemo. . . !

DOUG. But if he watches closely — !

NAOMI. *Him?!* He probably puts on a blindfold to take an *aspirin!*

DOUG. Aw . . . well . . .

NICKI. *Please*, Doug. . . ?

POOPSIE. *Humphrey Bogart* would have done it!

DOUG. (*tempted by the image*) Do you really *think* so, Poopsie?

POOPSIE. (*takes his hands*) I know so. And so do you. Any man who *looks* so much like Bogart would *feel* the way he did!

DOUG. But a person's looks have nothing to do with the way he — (*It belatedly hits him — and it feels marvelous.*) You think *I* look like *Bogart*?!

POOPSIE. You mean no one's ever *told* you that before?

DOUG. (*is really seeing her for the first time and liking what he sees*) No. I — I guess nobody ever really looked *closely* before!

POOPSIE. (*also liking what she sees*) The poor fools!

JASON. (*going crazy with anxiety, cannot hold silent*) Rick — Ilsa — that *plane* will leave without *all* of us!

DOUG. (*disengages his hands from POOPSIE's reluctantly*) He's right. I've — *got* to help him . . .

POOPSIE. (*smiling bravely*) I understand.

NICKI. (*as impatient as JASON*) Good, then let's get *on* with it! Okay?!

NAOMI. About time! Now, Mister Kingsley — you go to the coat-closet and —

POOPSIE. (*sniffing the air*) Hey, I smell something burning!

NAOMI. My *roast!* (*bolts for* K.R., *towing POOPSIE with her*) I'll get the oven-mitts, you grab the fire extinguisher! (*They exit.*)

DOUG. (*dismayed by POOPSIE's absence*) *Now* what do we do?!

NICKI. (*picks up suitcase, starts toward* B.R.) Just let me get this out of sight, then Jason can coax Thornton out of the closet — (*exits; JASON and DOUG look after her, uncertainly*)

JASON/DOUG. *And* — ?!

NICKI. (*off*) Wait a minute!

JASON. (*to DOUG*) We let him out and wait a minute?

NICKI. (*off*) *No!* Wait a minute for *me* to ditch this *suitcase!*

DOUG. (*calling off* B.R.) But what about that *hotel?*

JASON. *What* hotel?

DOUG. That I'm *taking* her to!

JASON. Over my dead body, you are!

DOUG. (*as they square off to do battle*) Now, *listen*, you — !

NICKI. (*entering briskly via* B.R., *minus suitcase*) Stop it, *both* of you! First let's solve the problems of Murdock, *then* you can solve the problem of *me!*

NAOMI. (*enters* K.R.) Poopsie's got things under control in the kitchen. Let's get Mister Murdock before his brains are *totally* fried, okay? (*starts for foyer, TRIO following*) It's only hot enough to fry an *egg* in the *living room* — inside that *closet* you could probably bake *pottery!* (*will position — via gesture — the group thusly, on her upcoming line: JASON at closet door, DOUG in* U.L. *corner between hall-and-closet doors, NICKI on*

*living room level just between two rails, and herself with
her back to* K.L., *all of them facing one another*) Now,
let's organize this thing—Mister Kingsley, you stand
here . . . Doctor Procter there . . . Miss Channing right
where she can guard against an escape to the living
room, and I'll bar the kitchen!

DOUG. What am *I* barring?

NAOMI. Nothing. You're hiding! Now, Mister
Kingsley, fake a farewell to the doctor—good and *loud*,
mind you, the closet has a thick door—and then let's all
do what comes naturally when Murdock emerges into
the trap!

JASON. But what do we *do* with him when we capture
him?

NAOMI. Immobilize him so he can get his *liniment-*
shot!

NICKI. Out *here*? The bedroom would be better—I
mean, he'll probably faint before we even get his shirt
off—!

JASON. That makes sense. Everybody ready—?
(*OTHERS nod.*) Okay, then, here goes. . . ! (*with
mouth near closet door, says loudly:*) WELL, *GOOD-
BYE*, DOCTOR PROCTER! SORRY YOU
COULDN'T STICK AROUND!

DOUG. (*leans to hall-door knob, opens door a frac-
tion, shouts:*) GOODBYE, KINGSLEY! IF YOU
EVER FIND MISTER MURDOCK, LET ME KNOW!
(*slams front door loudly; an instant later, closet-door
flings open [and is left at right angles to wall, thus
hiding* DOUG *from entrant's view], and* T.B. *rushes
eagerly, smiling hopefully, to center of foyer—his shirt
is unbuttoned to his waist, sleeves rolled up, face drip-
ping sweat, shirtfront totally soggy, hair wet and limp
and messed up, etc.*)

T.B. Thank *heaven* he's gone—! (*stops speaking abruptly, sensing something's wrong; panting hard, like an animal at bay, looks hard at NICKI [JASON, meanwhile, has eased his way to hall door and leaned back, slightly spread-eagled, against it], then swivels head and looks hard at NAOMI, then snaps his head fast to look at JASON—with each head-movement he becomes more fearful—and then, as if "seeing with his shoulder-blades", slowly turns his head to look into* u.l. *corner, as DOUG—matching movement with slow swivel of T.B.'s head—gently moves closet door* R., *fully exposing him to T.B.'s gaze as head-turn is completed; T.B. sees him, and shrieks in near-soprano:*) Oh, nooooo—! (*pivots instantly and rushes back toward closet just as door swings shut, and starts pounding on door with heels of fists, shrieking insanely:*) Let me in! Let me in! Help! Somebody! Anybody!

(*GROUP has descended upon him by now, DOUG taking his right arm, NAOMI his left arm, JASON his right ankle, and NICKI his left ankle, and they lift him bodily, and will move from foyer into living room and across to* B.R. *and finally exit via* B.R. *[carrying T.B. feet-first, so the last we'll see of him is his face—he's being toted in prone, not supine, position]; all this happens over following dialogue. SPECIAL NOTE: the speech by T.B. is* continuous, *and is given* during *the speeches that follow it; in other words, from the time he is picked up till he vanishes, he is sobbily whimpering the following speech; the toter-quartet will say their speeches back and forth to one another as if he were not saying a thing; in other words, think of T.B.'s upcoming speech as "background music" over*

*which our quartet chat as if not even paying atten-
tion to it.*)

T.B. (*"Muzak"*) No, please! Put me down! Wait!
Checks! Stop! I'd rather stay sick! I don't want that needle! Mercy! *Mercy!* Police! Anybody! It's gonna hurt, I
know it's gonna hurt, I can't *stand* being hurt, I don't
wanna be hurt, you're not *listening* to me, I want a second opinion, I'm having a nightmare, somebody wake
me up—*Mommeeeeee. . . !* (*and* during *his uninter-
rupted plea:*)

JASON. You won't even *feel* the needle, sir!

NAOMI. Doctor Procter is *very* gentle about it!

DOUG. I'll deaden the area before I even pick up the
needle!

NICKI. *I* feel just *fine!* Don't *you* want to feel fine?!
(*And they are gone; then, DOUG re-appears, goes to
sideboard where he left his medical bag when he arrived
the second time, gets the bag, and exits* B.R. *with it; all
this happens over:*)

T.B. (*off*) No, don't! Let me off this bed! Let *go* of
me! Wait! Listen! I'll make you rich! (*DOUG is onstage
now, moving to bag.*) You can have your weight in
gold—in diamonds—in lottery tickets! Isn't there
anything you want, something you've *always* wanted,
something you thought you could never have? I'll get it
for you, whatever it is! Mink coats! Lincoln Continen-
tals! (*DOUG is moving back and exiting* B.R. *now.*)
Your own penthouse! *Two* penthouses! I'll buy you *Tif-
fany's*! (*as DOUG apparently comes into his view:*) Oh,
no! Doctor! Don't open that bag! Don't take that needle
out! Stop rolling up my sleeve! No! No, don't!
Aaaaaaaaaah!

(*Silence; then NAOMI, DOUG, NICKI and JASON enter — in that order — via* B.R., *all of them looking exhausted-but-relieved.*)

NAOMI. I *told* you he'd pass out cold!

DOUG. I've never *seen* such strength in a man his age!

JASON. I need a drink!

NICKI. Me, too! I feel like Lady MacBeth just finishing up with *King Duncan!*

NAOMI. (*taking salad tray from sideboard*) I guess nobody's interested in hot salad, are they? (*will exit* K.R. *with tray, during:*)

NICKI. (*at table*) May as well get rid of the vichysoisse, too! (*She, DOUG and JASON will each take a soup-plate and place-setting and start toward* K.R. *with them.*)

POOPSIE. (*enters* K.R.) The fire is out.

JASON. (*as he and others pass her en route to kitchen*) How's the roast?

POOPSIE. Well, the next time you have a cookout, you won't have to buy charcoal! (*She moves to table as TRIO exits, picks up Steemo bottle.*) Shall I put the liniment in the bathroom?

NAOMI. (*entering* K.R.) I'll do that, Poopsie. Listen, you may as well give me that robe back now, too. (*POOPSIE dutifully hands bottle over, shucks out of robe, during:*)

POOPSIE. How's Mister Murdock?

NAOMI. Sleeping like a baby. And soon as he wakes up, we tell him he's cured, and then we can *all* relax!

POOPSIE. (*as NAOMI starts for* B.R. *with bottle and robe*) Say, listen, if *everybody's* supposed to be cured — why don't you put the *air-conditioning* back on?

JASON. (*just entering* K.R., *headed for bar*) A *marvelous* suggestion! Why didn't *I* think of that?! Mrs. Schuyler — ?

NAOMI. (*on brink of* B.R.-*exit, without turning:*) Will do! (*exits*)

JASON. (*fixing drinks*) What can I make for you, Poopsie? (*NICKI and DOUG will enter via* K.R. *during:*)

POOPSIE. Whatever everyone else is having, I guess. But make mine a short one. I have to work tomorrow. (*will move to sofa and sit near* L. *end, during:*)

DOUG. What do you *do*, anyhow, Poopsie?

POOPSIE. I'm a Television-Trip Guest.

NICKI. A what? (*DOUG and NICKI will gravitate* L., *he ending up beside POOPSIE on sofa, NICKI in armchair, while JASON makes four drinks, during:*)

POOPSIE. *You* know — like on a quiz show, when the emcee tells the winner, "We'll fly *you* and a *guest* to Kingston, Jamaica"? . . . Well, *I'm* the *guest*!

DOUG. But — *I* thought the winners got to pick their *own* guests?!

POOPSIE. (*nods, sighs*) That's what *everybody* thinks.

NAOMI. But why don't the quiz shows just send the *winner's* guest?

POOPSIE. It's cheaper using me: I fly tourist-class, take a bus from the airport instead of a taxi, don't order expensive meals at the hotel, sleep in one of the cheaper rooms — they must save a *fortune*!

DOUG. But — that's *horrible*!

POOPSIE. (*shrugs*) It's a living. (*JASON will deliver drinks to the group, and end up seated near* R. *end of sofa, near NICKI, during:*)

NICKI. But don't the winners *object* when they find their vacation's with a *stranger*?

POOPSIE. Would *you* turn down a free trip to the tropics for a silly reason like *that*?

NICKI. (*mulling it over*) You know — I'm not *sure* . . .

JASON. Do the winners ever complain?

POOPSIE. Oh, once in a while *some* of them do, but then the show offers them the equivalent of a tropical vacation for *one* in *money*, and they usually go away happy. Mostly, though, they figure what the hell and start packing.

NICKI. Wait a minute — you're working *tomorrow*? I didn't think *any* of those shows taped on the *weekend*. . . ?

POOPSIE. Oh, they don't. Tomorrow, I'm working a three-days-in-Bermuda trip.

JASON. But if you work Monday-through-Friday at those tapings, when do you get a day *off*?

POOPSIE. (*shrugs*) Every weekend! I mean, going to San Juan, Rio, Acapulco, Ocho Rios and Nassau isn't what you'd call *working*!

DOUG. (*nods with grudging comprehension*) I see what you mean!

NICKI. But what do you do when — I mean — do any of these men you travel with ever get *fresh*?

POOPSIE. (*dreamily*) If I'm lucky!

DOUG. (*shocked*) Poopsie!

POOPSIE. Not like *that*, silly! I mean, they decide to *escort* me around the tropical paradise — take me dining and dancing — buy me drinks — that's what *Alvin's* going to do!

JASON. Ah! You met your new boy friend on the *quiz show*!

POOPSIE. (*nods*) Yeah. It was *real* romantic! When he found out *I* was the guest he was taking, he even offered to get me a *first-class* airline ticket, so we could ride to Bermuda side-by-side, promised to get me a *suite* when we got to the hotel, and then he took me in his arms, pulled off his false beard, and—

NICKI. *Whoa*, gal! Wait a minute! Did I *miss* something, or—?

POOPSIE. Oh, you mean the *beard*? Well, you see, Alvin said he didn't want to be *recognized* when the show went on the air, so he got this beard and thick-rimmed glasses, and—

DOUG. Poopsie, this man might be a wanted *criminal*!

JASON. What does Alvin do when he's *not* going on quiz shows in disguise?

POOPSIE. (*shrugs*) I didn't *ask* him. I mean, his plans are so groovy, why should I louse them up by being *nosy*? (*ALL have their drinks by now, and JASON is seated.*)

NAOMI. (*enters* B.R., *minus bottle and robe*) Hey, I think our Sleeping Beauty is coming out of his faint! Better get ready for your bon-voyage speeches to him, folks. *I'm* going to turn on that *air-conditioner*! (*exits* K.R.)

JASON. (*raises glass, and each of the OTHERS will do same on their lines:*) Well, here's to cool air!

NICKI. Here's to Mister Murdock's departure!

POOPSIE. Here's to finally getting my hair washed!

DOUG. (*to POOPSIE, as Bogart-as-all-get-out:*) Here's looking at *you*, kid!

POOPSIE. (*wriggles and simpers with delight*) Oooo, Dougie!

(*ALL drink, and get to their feet during:*)

NAOMI. (*off*) I think this switch is stuck—the air-conditioner won't turn on!

POOPSIE. (*moves through* S.L. *toward* K.L. *on:*) Here, let *me* try—I used to *install* those things!

Doug. Really? You must be a lot smarter than you — (*catches himself, embarrassed*) I mean — to *look* at you, one would never think that — uh —

Poopsie. (*pauses at* k.l. *for:*) That I actually have a *brain*? . . . You'd be surprised! (*gives him a friendly wink, exits*)

Doug. (*turns to JASON and NICKI*) And I *would*, too!

Nicki. Doug — if I'm the only woman you'll ever love — how come you've never done Bogart for *me*?

Doug. (*sheepishly*) Aw, Nicki — it's just kind of *fun* doing it — I mean, no woman ever told me I *looked* like Bogart before.

Nicki. Doug — you *don't* look like Bogart!

Jason. Not even slightly!

Doug. (*patently disappointed*) Not even just a *little* bit?

Nicki. (*with gentle amusement*) Well — maybe beauty is in the eye of the beholder!

Naomi. (*peeks in* k.r.) Say, while Poopsie's fixing the thermostat, how about I make you all some sandwiches? I just took a closer look at the roast, and some of it's quite salvageable!

Jason. Marvelous! I'm starved!

Nicki. Same here!

Doug. Likewise!

Naomi. I'll get right on it! (*vanishes into kitchen again*)

Doug. (*moving* d.l.) Mind if I put on the TV?

Jason. Be my guest. Anything good on, tonight?

Nicki. Well, let's see — it's Friday evening — what time is it?

Doug. (*has TV on, now [sound muted and low], is fiddling with dial*) I'll flip around the channels and see . . . (*T.B. enters slowly via* b.r.; *his face has been dried, and his hair is no longer a mess, and he's fastening his cuff-buttons.*)

NICKI. Mister Murdock! How are you feeling? (*She and JASON move toward him.*)

T.B. (*with chagrin*) A lot better than I *deserve* to feel! Boy, what an idiot I was!

NICKI. Nonsense! *Lots* of people are afraid of needles!

T.B. Oh, I don't mean *that* part — I mean the way I let myself get so *excited* about it! Imagine, someone infected with LaBeck's Syndrome getting into a state like that! I'm lucky I didn't blow up all over your living room!

JASON. Say, I'd completely *forgotten* about *that* danger! Yes, you certainly *were* lucky! (*Over dialogue, NICKI, JASON and T.B. will move more-and-less aimlessly into area just below foyer.*)

NICKI. Naomi's making sandwiches — would you like one? It's not the big dinner you were expecting, but —

T.B. Thank you, Lavinia, that would be most kind of you.

NICKI. (*steps up into foyer, starts for* K.L.) I'll just go tell her — (*Then she stops, and ALL react as DOOR-BELL rings; T.B., of course, is only normally curious, but OTHERS onstage go wide-eyed with terror.*)

JASON. (*over-loudly, as if sheer volume could mask the already-heard doorbell*) What would you like on that sandwich?!

NICKI. (*catching JASON's drift, takes T.B.'s arm, tries to lead him* K.L. *as she expounds as loudly as JASON:*) We've got ketchup, mustard, horseradish, pickle relish — ! (*DOORBELL again*)

T.B. (*mildly resisting NICKI's tugs at his arm*) Isn't anybody going to *answer* that?

JASON/NICKI/DOUG. (*in pseudo-innocent unison:*) Answer *what*?!

T.B. (*a bit uneasy*) The—the *doorbell*, of course!

JASON. *I* didn't hear the doorbell! (*DOORBELL*) I didn't hear it *again*!

T.B. (*palm-to-forehead, as if checking for fever*) I'm *hallucinating*!

NICKI. Now-now, what you need is a nice sandwich! (*tries leading him K.L. again, but he resists, shakes off her hand*)

T.B. (*to DOUG*) You said that shot would *cure* me!

DOUG. (*extemporizing hopelessly*) Well—uh—these things take *time* . . . (*DOORBELL*)

T.B. Aaargh! I *know* I heard the bell! I *can't* be crazy! I'm *not* hallucinating! (*lurches to hall door and yanks it open before anyone can prevent it, then stares into hall, gives a moaning scream, staggers backward to where NICKI can grab and support him as his knees start to buckle, and then VONGA—a comely young lady clad in a sort of fir kirtle, with feather-circlets around wrists and ankles, a boar's-tooth necklace, and wampum-beaded headband, carrying a spear, steps in and stands there*) *Who* are *you*?!

VONGA. Vonga, the Jungle Girl!

T.B. (*wide-eyed shock*) I *am* crazy! This is a nightmare! Look at her! Just *look* at her!

JASON/NICKI/DOUG. (*with limp conviction, because anything's worth a try:*) Look at *who*?

T.B. (*abruptly galvanized rushes toward coat-closet on:*) I've got to get out of here! At least I can die at home in my own bed!

[*NOTE: A lot will happen very quickly here, so pay close attention: T.B. will yank open closet door and dash inside, moving* L. *out of our view briefly; even as he is opening closet door, NAOMI steps in* K.L., *reacts to VONGA (her niece, of course), and VONGA brightens and smiles and starts toward her aunt as if about to speak, but NAOMI puts a finger to her lips (her own lips, not VONGA's), takes her arm, and leads her off via* K.L., *even as JASON lunges to shut hall door fast, but without slamming it, and then T.B. — carrying his jacket, tie and vest which he'd left in closet when he first hid there — comes scurrying out of closet, stops dead, looks upon the forced smiles of each conspirator, from one to the other, in something of a daze, and then:*]

T.B. Where did she go?

TRIO. Where did *who* go?

T.B. Vonga the Jungle Girl!

TRIO. *Who* — ?!

T.B. You *must* have seen her! She rang the bell, and — (*stops, reacts, as LIGHTS DIM, FLICKER, THEN COME BACK UP FULL*) What was *that*?!

JASON. (*goes to him*) Nothing, sir! Really!

T.B. But I saw — ?!

JASON. I mean, nothing to *worry* about! The lights *always* do that when the *air-conditioner* kicks in! Now that we've all had our shots, we don't have to worry about the —

T.B. Maybe *you* don't! But I *still* don't feel cured!

NICKI. You're just *hunger*-crazed! Let me get you that sandwich! (*exits* K.L.)

T.B. Doctor! Aren't we kind of — jumping the gun? I mean, shouldn't we all be *tested*, or something, to be sure we *are* cured before we risk cooling the air in here?!

Doug. (*near* l. *rail, still on living-room level*) Nothing to worry about, sir. The three of you have *all* had your Steemo-shots, and I promise you there's nothing more to fear. According to the hospital — and I checked it out *thoroughly* with the medics there before I came by — the cure is downright instantaneous, with no side-effects or other repercussions.

T.B. (*heels of hands to temples*) But why am I hearing doorbells and seeing jungle-girls?!

JASON. You just got *up* too soon, is all. Doug *did* say you should have two hours' bed-rest, after getting your shot. Believe me, you're going to feel *just* fine. Give it time.

T.B. But that's only a *layman's* opinion!

Doug. Then listen to *me*. I'm a doctor! Jason's right. Just sit down and relax. Everything's going to be just fine! (*moves back toward TV to channel-dial some more*)

T.B. Well — perhaps you're right . . . (*shivers slightly*) That *air*-conditioning feels *awful* against this damp shirt, though — (*starts slipping into vest, moves after JASON, who has stepped down into living-room area, now, but pauses still on foyer-level directly between rails to start buttoning vest, as NICKI enters* K.R.)

NICKI. Everything's under control in the kitchen! (*JASON and DOUG smile with relief, but T.B. gives her a puzzled look, so she adds quickly:*) I mean, Naomi's almost finished making the sandwiches!

T.B. Oh, good!

NICKI. (*in sideboard area*) Can I fix you a drink while you're waiting, Thornton?

T.B. Thank you, Lavinia. I could *use* one right about now! (*his left hand prods his right armpit on:*) I'm *still* sore from that inoculation!

(*TRIO exchange amused looks at the power of his
    imagination, and then DOUG finds a program to
    his liking and turns up TV-volume [we'll hear some
    prime-time Friday-night network show in progress—
    or even* see *it, if your screen is audience-visible and
    you own a VCR]; DOUG moves back to sit on* L.
    *sofa-arm and sip his drink as NICKI finishes mak-
    ing drink and starts for T.B. with it, and T.B. [if
    done buttoning vest] starts slipping into his suit-
    jacket, and ALL are idly watching the TV screen
    . . . and* then:)

ANNOUNCER ON TV. (*with VCR-visuals, if you've got
'em*) We interrupt this regularly scheduled program for
a news bulletin! (*ALL perk up interest slightly.*) The
man who so elated medical science this morning with his
miraculous recovery from a supposedly incurable
disease, LaBeck's Syndrome—(*Now the group's eye-
contact with the screen is* intense, *and patently fearful
[T.B.'s fear, of course, for a different reason from the
OTHERS'], and even NAOMI and VONGA creep in,*
K.L., *upstage of and unseen by T.B. to Hear The Worst,
during:*)—has just been found dead in his hospital bed
by a candy-striper who had entered to pick up his
supper-tray. Doctors are baffled by this unexpected turn
of events, but until an autopsy has been completed they
urge *anyone* with this illness *not* to attempt the supposedly harmless cure! (*T.B.'s hand goes to his armpit
again, his face a mask of horror.*) Repeat: Do *not*
attempt—

(*DOUG, however, has abruptly snapped out of his
    panicky paralysis and has dived at the TV, snapping
    it off in mid-sentence, now; but it's far too late:*

T.B., his eyes rolling up into his head, topples for-
ward in a dead faint, into the arms of JASON and
NICKI [who dashes there in the nick of time, start-
ing her move on the words ". . . harmless cure"]; the
visual-effect, quick as 1-2-3-4, is 1) NAOMI/
VONGA enter, 2) NICKI dashes for T.B., 3) DOUG
dives for TV, and 4) T.B. topples; these should occur
in quick sequence, none of the moves simultaneous,
for optimal comedic effect; pause one beat after
topple, with ALL onstage looking toward T.B.;
then JASON turns his gaze toward DOUG, and:)

JASON. If you're not busy Monday, care to join me
job-hunting. . . ?

THE CURTAIN FALLS

End of Act Two

ACT THREE

*About fifteen minutes later. Curtain-rise finds JASON
seated at* L. *end of sofa, NICKI seated about* C. *of
sofa. Closet door has been closed. BOTH are star-
ing Out Front, slightly dazed; they are not glassy-
eyed, but not far from it. Each is alone with his/her
thoughts on recent events, and not too happy about
them. After a moment, NAOMI enters via* B.R. *and
stops just inside room. Sensing her presence,
JASON and NICKI slowly turn their gazes her way
and just stare at her in silence; then:*

NAOMI. He's sleeping quite peacefully now . . . (*No
response; she moves another pace toward them, stops,
and:*) That sedative really worked well . . . (*No
response; she moves another pace nearer sofa, stops,
and:*) It calmed his hysterics like a miracle when he
came out of his faint . . . (*same business; her stop this
time is just short of* S.R. *area*) Maybe I'm not *telling* this
right . . . are there any *questions*? (*NICKI slowly
swivels her head to look at JASON, then slowly swivels
it back to face NAOMI again; when BOTH are once
more facing her:*)

BOTH. (*in incredulous unison:*) "*Vonga* the *Jungle
Girl*"—?!

NAOMI. (*relieved to finally realize what's bemusing
them*) Oh, *that*!

NICKI. *Yes!*

JASON. *That!*

NAOMI. (*shrugs, moves to sit in armchair*) Well, I *told*
you she was in *show business*! (*sits*)

JASON. I thought you meant a *stage* actress—or at
least daytime TV—!

NICKI. What *is* she with — a traveling *circus*?

NAOMI. She entertains at Shriner's conventions.

JASON. And you *picked* her to play my *wife*?!

NAOMI. I didn't *know* she'd show up in her *working* clothes!

NICKI. Why *did* she, for heaven's sake?!

NAOMI. It was a perfectly understandable error —

JASON. She thought I lived in a *tree*?

NAOMI. *I* told her to come over and I might have a short-term *job* for her. I guess she thought this would be an *audition*!

NICKI. Why didn't you tell her what *kind* of job?

NAOMI. Because she was *out* when I phoned! And I could *hardly* give the details to the hotel's *message* clerk, could I?! . . . "Hurry *over*, honey, my *boss* needs a *wife* for the night!'"?

JASON. (*must admit reluctantly*) Well — that *would* be a lot to lay on the man . . . but how in the world did she *get* here? (*to NICKI*) I can't *imagine* where she'd carry *bus* fare!

NAOMI. Her hotel's only a few blocks away. She probably walked. In New York City, who'd pay any attention?

NICKI. I'd think she'd worry about being grabbed by a weirdo!

JASON. Not while she's carrying that *spear*!

NAOMI. She knows how to *use* it, too; a girl learns a *lot* of things at Shriner's conventions.

JASON. Say, by the way, what's her *real* name?

NAOMI. That *is* her real name.

NICKI. "Vonga the Jungle Girl"?!

JASON. What's your sister's married name — "Jungle" or "Girl"?

NAOMI. It's like this: My sister and her husband were

African missionaries; one day, while they were out proselytizing, they came upon this little girl who'd somehow wandered off into the wild, years before, and had been raised by a herd of ostriches — except she didn't really much enjoy burying her face in the sand to hunt for bugs and grubs, so she was quite happy to return with them to their compound, and —

JASON. I don't think I want to hear any more, Mrs. Schuyler.

NAOMI. I never *said* it was a *pretty* story.

(*Then ALL look up as VONGA enters via* K.R., *minus her spear, but with a fairly meaty beef bone which she is happily munching upon; she moves to* S.R. *area wordlessly, sits on* R. *arm of sofa, continues to munch.*)

NICKI. (*after a pause*) What — what does Vonga *do* at these conventions, Naomi?

NAOMI. Arm-wrestles all contenders.

JASON. I *really* don't want to —

NAOMI. Never *loses*, either.

JASON. (*a bit testily*) — *hear* any more!

NAOMI. (*not sorry*) Sorry.

DOUG. (*ALL look up again, even VONGA, toward* B.R. *as DOUG enters and goes to phone; he picks up receiver, but before he dials, he looks toward silent group in sofa-area and observes dryly:*) Who's got the Tupperware?

NICKI. Don't make jokes, Doug. What are we going to *do*?!

DOUG. I'm going to call the hospital and find out about that guy who kicked off.

VONGA. (*stops munching long enough to remark:*) Vonga *like* football!

NAOMI. No, dear, Doctor Procter means the man who *died.*

VONGA. Why doctor not *say* so?

JASON. Doug's always lapsing into *scientific* terminology. (*DOUG scowls at JASON, starts dialing phone.*)

NICKI. (*will rise and move partway toward DOUG during:*) Doug, what possible *good* will it do to find out *what* killed the poor man? We're *still* faced with the problem of un-panicking *Thornton* when he wakes up.

DOUG. (*awaiting his call to go through*) I'm just hoping there were "special circumstances" about the guy's death—you know, *complications* that caused it, things that needn't worry Mister Murdock at all . . .

JASON. The way *my* luck's running, whatever *he* had, T.B. will *also* have—in spades! *Then* what do we do?

NAOMI. (*rises from armchair*) Don't be so *negative,* Mister Kingsley—your luck's *bound* to change sooner or later! (*starts toward* K.R.) I've got to clean up that mess Poopsie left by the thermostat!

DOUG. Can't *she* clean it up?

NAOMI. She went home to wash her hair while you were attending our patient.

DOUG. (*visibly disappointed*) Without even saying goodbye?!

NICKI. Don't worry about it, Rick—you'll *always* have *Paris!*

DOUG. (*He looks about ready to snarl some reply, but abruptly gets his party on phone, so gives it up; NAOMI will exit to kitchen, VONGA will finish munching and exit shortly after her, and NICKI will drift back into* S.R. *area, remaining standing, during DOUG's stint on the phone:*) Hello? . . . Yes, this is Douglas Procter; I use your facilities for our corporation's annual physicals—. . . Yes, that's right. I wanted to speak with the

doctor in charge of that patient who recently died—
the one with LaBeck's Syndrome—? . . . Oh, he did?
Well, when is he expected back? . . . Oh, damn . . .
No, I guess I'll have to try again—unless *you* could give
me the information I need? . . . Well, basically, I
wanted to find out the results of the autopsy . . . The
cause of death, yes . . . Uh-huh . . . Uh-huh . . . *What?!*
(*His mood shifts so suddenly to one of relieved elation
that NICKI and JASON both focus on him, JASON
coming hopefully to his feet.*) You're *sure* about that? . . .
Of *course* I sound relieved! I *am* relieved! . . . Yes,
thanks very much, I really appreciate it! (*hangs up
phone, turns toward his expectant eavesdroppers*)

NICKI. *Well*—?

JASON. What did you find *out*?

DOUG. Something that's going to make Mister Murdock *very* happy, *indeed*!

NICKI. Well, how about laying some of that happiness
on *us*!?

JASON. Yeah, what did that guy have that Mister Murdock couldn't *possibly* have?

DOUG. A birth certificate! (*DOUG, NICKI and
JASON will converge just below* K.R., *during:*)

NICKI. Come on, Doug, Thornton may have his *in-
human* side, but surely he was *born*!

DOUG. *Not* in eighteen-eighty-six!

[*NOTE: Since this is being written in 1985, you should
emend that 1886 date accordingly, depending upon
what year you* do *the show, so the following line
will be mathematically accurate:*]

JASON. He was *ninety-nine* years *old*?!

DOUG. A minor detail they omitted from that news
bulletin!

NICKI. So *that's* what he died of — *not* the Steemo-injection?

DOUG. I guess it was a slow news-day!

JASON. It's the last time I watch *that* network!

NAOMI. (*emerges* K.R.) What's all the excitement?

NICKI. That guy in the news bulletin died of old age!

JASON. He was pushing the century-mark!

DOUG. So we're *all* off the hook! When Murdock wakes up, we tell him he has nothing to worry about!

NICKI. Till age ninety-nine!

JASON. It's perfect! We both keep our jobs, Monica and I can get married, our boss thinks of Doug as the man who saved his life — (*to DOUG*) — I envy you your Christmas bonus! (*to ALL*) — and Steemo becomes a prescription drug and makes the company a *fortune!*

DOUG. (*elated*) I've *got* to tell Poopsie! (*starts toward foyer, abruptly stops*) *I* don't know where she *lives!*

NICKI. (*dryly*) Aren't you going to say goodbye to the only girl you'll ever love?

DOUG. What — ? *Oh!* Aw — Nicki — I don't know what to say — I mean — well —

NICKI. (*laughs*) Just say "congratulations" on my up-coming trip to Connecticut and get *out* of here!

DOUG. (*sincerely*) You're a beautiful person, Nicki.

NICKI. And don't you ever forget it!

JASON. (*starts toward desk*) I've got Poopsie's address in the desk, let me write it down for you —

NAOMI. Excuse me — (*OTHERS look her way.*) I hate to pull the rug out from under this Happy Ending, but aren't you all forgetting something — ?!

TRIO. *What?*

NAOMI. That *needle* Mister Murdock will forever believe he got in his *armpit*, that's what! Do you all recall *why* he had to get that imaginary shot?

JASON. To save his *life*, of course!

NICKI. Or *supposedly* save it, after being exposed to LaBeck's Syndrome—*also* supposedly.

NAOMI. Which Doctor Procter told him was *highly contagious*!

DOUG. It *is* highly contagious!

NAOMI. But that's exactly my point!

JASON. *What* is?

NAOMI. As soon as that terrified rabbit in the bedroom recovers *some* use of his mental faculties, it's gonna occur to him that Mister Kingsley has been exposed to that disease for *years*—and has been happily going to *work* with all those lovely *germs* all over him—and infecting the entire *staff* of Murdock and Moran—!

(*In rapid succession:*)

DOUG. Oh, boy!

NAOMI. Oh, damn!

JASON. Oh, nuts!

NAOMI. But Doctor Procter can't *possibly* fake giving *all* the necessary inoculations, the company's too big—so everyone will have to *get* those armpit-shots—and so will their friends and families—and when the word gets out, what with *hundreds* of people supposedly carriers of this dread disease, the city will have to declare a medical *emergency*, and those "eight million stories in the Naked City" are all going to have *very* sore armpits—and, tell me now, *what* do you suppose will happen to *this* merry little group if it ever *emerges* that the whole thing was a big fat *lie*?!

JASON. (*shaken*) Holy Toledo—we'll be lucky if they let us off with a simple *lynching*!

DOUG. They'll be likelier to have us burned at the stake!

NICKI. But what are we going to *do*?! We *can't* tell
Thornton he's *not* cured—but if we tell him he *is* cured,
and he starts *thinking* about what Naomi said—?!

JASON. Mrs. Schuyler—what *can* we do?!

NAOMI. Sorry. *My* job is *presenting* problems.
Somebody *else* will have to *solve* them!

DOUG. (*moves a step downstage of group, wringing
hands*) This is ghastly! Today a successful corporate
doctor—

JASON. —Tomorrow a human sacrifice in Times
Square!

NICKI. But—Thornton Murdock wouldn't want the
publicity of starting a city-wide medical epidemic—.
would he—?

JASON. (*shrugs*) His secretary once took home one of
the office staplers. He called the F.B.I.

DOUG. I remember that—luckily, her purse was
snatched on the subway so the case was dismissed for
lack of evidence. (*By now, TRIO has re-grouped
downstage of NAOMI.*)

NICKI. This is all like a bad dream!

JASON. Hey! That's it! This *is* all a bad dream!

NICKI. If you *believe* that, you *are* dreaming!

JASON. Not *my* dream—*Murdock's*!

DOUG. So what are *we*—figments of his imagination?!

JASON. No-no, not *us*—just everything that's *happened* here tonight!

NICKI. (*becoming hopefully excited*) Do you
mean—?!

DOUG. (*similarly*) We try to convince him that—?!

JASON. He believed he got a hypo—he believed he met
Vonga the Jungle Girl—why wouldn't he believe he
fainted from the heat during the vichysoisse and *dreamed*
everything?!

NICKI. But what about Lavinia's contagious disease?! We'll be back to *that* again!

DOUG. *Not* if I tell him he's got Natural Immunity to it! And Jason has, too! That way, we'll also avoid starting a city-wide medical emergency!

JASON. It's certainly worth a try. What do *you* think, Monica?

NICKI. I'm game if you are!

DOUG. So, if nobody has a *better* plan — ?

NAOMI. *I* have a better plan. (*steps downstage to join group* — none *of whom is looking toward* B.R. *as a frazzled T.B. appears in archway, a crushed and dying man — at least, until he hears:*)

TRIO. What?

NAOMI. Tell Mister Murdock the *truth*!

JASON. *What?!* Tell him that I *lied* on my employment application, that I've never even *been* married, that Monica was only *pretending* to be Lavinia, and his trusted corporate doctor went *along* with us on it?!

DOUG. Not to mention convincing him he was hallucinating, terrifying him with that needle, pretending to give him a shot of liniment in the armpit — (*T.B.'s hand goes automatically to his armpit, then withdraws, and his manner is no longer hangdog; his eyes are steely, and if any of the group onstage happened to* look *into those eyes at this moment, they would* die.) — bullying him, sedating him, and lying to him for two solid hours?!

NICKI. (*after a gloomy pause*) *Maybe* if you waited till he was in a *good mood*, and — ?

NAOMI. The truth's the *only* way! You're all getting in deeper and deeper, and — !

JASON. No! We can pull off the dream-thing! I know it! We fooled him once, and we can fool him again!

NICKI. I *know* we can do it, darling! I hope.

DOUG. There's just *one* thing we'll have to avoid, though! (*OTHERS* — including *T.B.* — *lean slightly forward to him, all ears.*)

OTHERS EXCEPT T.B. *What?*

DOUG. The *second opinion* he kept shouting about earlier. *Whatever* we do, we mustn't let him go to a *hospital!*

NAOMI. Why *not?*

DOUG. Because they'll check his condition — they'll find he's never been *exposed* to LaBeck's Syndrome — and they'll *certainly* tell him he hasn't got *Natural Immunity* to it!

JASON. That's enough reasons for *me!*

NICKI. (*nods vigorously*) *I'm* sold! (*With a taut, frightening smile, T.B.* — *keeping a watchful eye on the group, eases himself backward and out of view; he's obviously Up To Something.*)

NAOMI. Well — I'm against it — but I'll do whatever I can to help, of course.

JASON. Thanks, Mrs. Schuyler, you're a treasure!

NAOMI. Oh, speaking of treasure — (*takes something from her pocket, holds it out*) Poopsie forgot her *friendship* ring in the kitchen — she took it off when she was fixing the thermostat.

DOUG. (*reaches for it*) *I'll* take it back to her — (*When OTHERS stare at him, he adds, guiltily:*) I mean, *if* her place is on my way *home*, of course.

NAOMI. It certainly *ought* to be — she lives on the next floor down.

DOUG. (*to JASON*) But *you* were going to give me her *address* — ?!

JASON. Her *apartment* number, is what I meant.

DOUG. Well, which apartment — (*stops as he takes*

really good look at ring he holds) Hey! Did you say "*friendship* ring"? With sapphires and diamonds?!

NAOMI. (*shrugs*) I guess Alvin is *very* friendly!

JASON. Aha! Then we were *right* about Alvin, I'll bet! Not showing his face on TV, having this much money to throw around—

NICKI. Yeah! I'll bet he *is* a gangster!

NAOMI. (*incredulous*) Poopsie's new boy friend—a *gangster*?

JASON. (*shrugs*) Why *not*? Your *niece* is an *ostrich*!

DOUG. Say, if he *is* a gangster, I wonder if I could talk Poopsie into having *him* take care of Mister Murdock?!

JASON. You can't *do* that!

NICKI. Why *not*?

JASON. T.B. will be coming out of that bedroom any minute—what if Alvin lives crosstown?!

NAOMI. Say, if he's due to come out *here*, I'd better send *Vonga* on her way! (*starts* K.R.) You'll *never* convince him he dreamed the whole thing if *she* strolls into view! (*exits* K.R.)

NICKI. (*as TRIO football-huddles*) Now, let's go over the plan in detail and get all our stories straight—(*Then they look up as VONGA enters via* K.R. *and heads toward* B.R., *with NAOMI following a pace behind.*)

VONGA. Vonga must get spear from bedroom!

JASON. (*stops her with:*) But you *can't*! He might be *just* waking up!

NAOMI. Well, we certainly can't *leave* it there! He'll *know* he's not imagining *that*!

NICKI. How did it *get* in there, anyhow?!

NAOMI. When he fainted in the foyer, Vonga helped us *carry* him there, remember?

DOUG. (*starts* B.R.) Let *me* get it! I'm a doctor—we're *trained* to hide things from patients! (*almost exits* B.R.—*then stops in terror as he hears:*)

T.B. (*off*) Doctor?! Kingsley?! Where *is* everybody!
Doug. (*whirls to face group*) He's *coming*!

JASON. *Hide*, Vonga, *hide*! (*and VONGA rushes via
S.R. to armchair, facing it, sits on R. end of coffeetable,
bends forward, lifts cushion, puts her head under it, and
just remains there, very still, her old ostrich-training
coming to the fore; OTHERS stand and stare at this
"head-in-the-sand" sight for a second, then JASON
heaves a mighty sigh, rushes to her, grabs her arm and
pulls her upright, on:*) No, not there!

VONGA. Why?

JASON. Because that's the *first* place he'd *look*! (*drags
her toward foyer*) Out in the hall! That's much safer!
We'll *mail* you your spear!

NICKI. You can't send her out on New York streets
like *that* without her *spear*!

JASON. She was raised by *ostriches*—she can *outrun*
the weirdos! (*DOORBELL; ALL freeze in panic; then:*)
The closet, quick!

T.B. (*off*) Kingsley? Lavinia? Anybody? (*JASON
shoves VONGA into closet, shuts door, then dives for
hall door just as DOORBELL RINGS AGAIN, and
yanks door open; POOPSIE, in a cute bathrobe/slipper
combination, her head towel-wrapped as after a sham-
pooing strides in smilingly, crossing directly to K.L. on:*)

POOPSIE. I forgot my friendship ring! (*As she exits
K.L., NAOMI grabs ring from DOUG and lurches to
K.R. on:*)

NAOMI. I'll take care of her—you take care of Murdock! (*She has barely vanished when T.B. enters via
B.R., simultaneous with a tightly smiling JASON
bounding from foyer to living-room level, and then trying to just stand there with savoir-faire and aplomb,
on:*)

JASON. Ah! Feeling better, sir?!

T.B. (*looking only pseudo-frazzled now, his eyes casting deadly glances whenever he's sure they're not looking*) I don't know. I feel dizzy, kind of wrung out—as if I'm just awakening from a *bad dream. . . !* (*OTHERS exchange look of elation which he feigns not to notice.*)

Doug. That's *wonderful!* Uh—that is—

Nicki. That you woke *up* from it, he means!

T.B. I hope I haven't spoiled the dinner-party . . . do you know—I can't remember *anything* since we started on the vichysoisse! (*OTHERS exchange* second *look of elation at this apparent stroke of luck.*)

Jason. (*with inane delight*) And *who* could *blame* you?! (*Faking or not, T.B. can hardly let this weird statement go unchallenged, and DOUG and NICKI realize this even as:*)

T.B. You *expect* your housekeeper's cooking to cause *memory*-lapses?

Jason. (*thinks hard; then, desperately:*) Once you've tasted *her* cooking, you *forget* everybody else's!

(*And by now, DOUG and NICKI each have grabbed T.B. by an arm, and start moving him sofaward, on:*)

Doug. Don't try to figure it out, sir, you've had quite an ordeal!

Nicki. What you need is to sit down and relax! (*They will get him to sofa and seat him, center, NICKI sitting on his left, DOUG on his right, during:*)

Jason. (*sees NAOMI emerging k.r., scurries to her for a* sotto voce *conversation:*) What did you tell Poop-sie?!

Naomi. To stay in the kitchen till we get your *boss* out

of here! The fewer extra people we have to explain, the better!

JASON. Good thinking! But you'd better get back in there and keep an eye on her, just in case!

NAOMI. What about my thirty-seven cents?

JASON. *What* thirty-seven cents?

NAOMI. The Steemo was five-thirty-seven. Mister Murdock only gave me *five*.

JASON. You'd blow my career for thirty-seven cents?!

NAOMI. Well, a penny here, a penny there . . . (*JASON grimaces in chagrin, gives her an exasperated dismissive wave of his hand, and heads for sofa, while NAOMI shrugs and exits* K.R.)

T.B. What *time* is it anyhow? I feel as though I've been here *forever*!

JASON. (*arriving in* S.R. *area, blurts sincerely:*) I know what you *mean*!

T.B. *What's* that you say?!

NICKI. (*instantly*) He means time sure doesn't fly when you're having no fun!

T.B. (*pretends to accept this, then — as if just noticing — remarks:*) Say — why is it so *cool* in here? And where is your *robe*, Lavinia?

NICKI. Uh!

JASON. Uh!

DOUG. (*since it's obviously up to him*) While you were sacking out, I *cured* her! She's a normal person at last!

NICKI. (*when T.B. looks her way, can think of nothing else but to smile giddily, fling her arms out and trumpet:*) Ta-DAAA!

T.B. That's wonderful news, my dear. Of course, you'll be checking into a hospital for *tests*, now, just to be *certain* — ?

JASON. She will? . . . I mean, she *will*!

DOUG. Uh—yes, *naturally*!

T.B. *Won't* it be a relief to know for *sure*! No more doubts, no more fears—!

NICKI. (*not too keenly*) Oh, golly, yes.

T.B. Will you be leaving soon?

NICKI. Uh—well, *reasonably* soon . . .

DOUG. (*hastily*) Soon as she feels *strong* enough!

JASON. Could take *hours*!

NICKI. *Lots* of hours!

T.B. (*feigns disappointment*) Oh, what a shame. I was hoping to offer you a *lift*! I mean, long as I'm heading that way *anyhow*—

DOUG. (*with dread*) You *are*?

T.B. Well, of *course* I am. Aren't *you*?

DOUG. *Me?*

T.B. *All* of you!

JASON. (*painfully, his heart in his throat*) *All* of us, sir?

T.B. Isn't LaBeck's Syndrome highly *contagious*?

NICKI. Well, *yes*, but—

T.B. And haven't we all been *exposed* to it?

JASON. Well, *yes*, but—

T.B. So shouldn't we make sure we're not *carriers* of the disease?

DOUG. Well, *yes*, but—

T.B. But *what*?

DOUG. (*thinks; then:*) It's *way* past our bedtime!

T.B. (*seems to accept this, to their surprise*) Yes. Yes, you're *quite* right, of course. Tomorrow *would* be much better. (*Then their brief relief is dashed as he continues:*) *Who* is sleeping *where*?

NICKI. (*very apprehensive*) *How's* that again?

T.B. Well, *obviously* we can't take the chance of spreading *infection*. We should all stay *here* tonight, and then go to the hospital *together*, in the morning.

JASON. (*hollowly*) What fun!

(*Unnoticed by them, VONGA slips out of closet, flits off via* K.L., *and then creeps furtively out via* K.R., *then does a* fast *getting-those-knees-up* tiptoe *toward* B.R., *exiting that way even as a belated and frantic NAOMI pops out* K.R. *too late to stop her; NAOMI stands there, irresolute and panicky, and then realizes what she is hearing as the dialogue continues without pause from JASON's line.*)

T.B. Now, of course, Jason and Lavinia will share their *own* bed—

NICKI. (*with a woeful exchange of glances with JASON*) What fun!

T.B. I can use the sofa, and Doctor Procter can curl up in the armchair—(*This next line is what captures NAOMI's distracted attention:*)—but *where* will Mrs. *Schuyler* sleep?!

NAOMI. Here, now, what's all this—?!

JASON. (*turns toward her, his smile sickly*) Mister Murdock thinks we should all have our hospital checkup *together*.

NAOMI. *What* hospital checkup?

T.B. (*stands*) To make certain none of us are carrying *contagion* around with us!

NAOMI. (*draws herself up proudly*) Well, *I'm* not carrying any!

T.B. You can't be *sure* of that—

NAOMI. 'Course I can! Wouldn't *work* here if it was *dangerous*! Luckily—(*She finishes with a triumphant smile.*)—*I* have Natural Immunity! (*turns tail and parades proudly off* K.R.)

T.B. But—!

JASON. (*seeing the "out" for* all *of them*) And so do *I*!

DOUG. (*springs to his feet*) Me, too!

NICKI. (*springs to her feet*) And *I'm* already *cured*!

T.B. (*frustrated, reverts to Danger Area again:*) Oh — very well, then — I'll just have to go *alone*, I guess!

TRIO. (*in terrified unison*) But you *can't*!

DOUG. (*before T.B. can comment*) That is, you don't *have* to! *You* have Natural Immunity, *too*!

NICKI. Doug tested you while you were asleep!

JASON. We were saving it as a surprise!

(*From* B.R., *VONGA enters, creeping slowly, keeping wary eye on T.B., now carrying her spear; she is just above table when T.B. spots her.*)

T.B. And what's *this — another* surprise?! (*Even as OTHERS start to turn that way, VONGA instantly spins to face table, lifts upstage edge of cloth, and ducks her head under it.*)

JASON. (*with the persistence of the Doomed*) What's *what*?

T.B. The creature with the *spear*!

NICKI. (*as if constant denial will make everything all right*) *What* creature?

DOUG. (*similarly*) *What* spear?

NAOMI. (*peeks out* K.R., *reacts, takes step into room, stops*) *I* don't see anybody *either*!

T.B. (*He is now just upstage of* S.R. *area, OTHERS between him and VONGA.*) I suppose you're going to tell me this is another *hallucination* — ?!

JASON. Yes! That's *exactly* what it is!

NICKI. (*lays a hand on JASON's arm*) Wait a minute! If he doesn't remember anything since the vichysoisse, how does he know about the hallucination-bit?!

T.B. (*smiling sardonically, his eyes like cold steel*) *Or* about Vonga the Jungle Girl — or about that needle in the armpit — or that news bulletin on the TV — ?

DOUG. Well, *that* you don't have to *worry* about!

T.B. The news bulletin? Why not?

JASON. You're too *young* to die!

T.B. Huh?

NICKI. The patient died of being ninety-nine years old!

NAOMI. *Not* from the *Steemo*!

JASON. So our product is *safe* to use!

DOUG. It'll make our company a *fortune*!

T.B. (*with deadly meaning*) *Our* product? *Our* company?

JASON. Oh, sir —

DOUG. You don't mean —

T.B. Oh, *don't* I now! (*As he enumerates their sins, OTHERS — excepting VONGA — slowly and very visibly shrivel and shrink and grimace in sick apprehension.*) *Lying* to me . . . *manhandling* me . . . *terrifying* me . . . convincing me I was going to *die* . . . going to get shot full of *liniment* . . . going *bananas* — !

VONGA. (*straightens into view again, with happy smile*) Vonga *like* bananas!

T.B. (*steps up between rails onto foyer-level, the better to tower over the miscreants as he rages:*) On your knees! *All* of you! (*ALL EXCEPT NICKI drop to knees, hands clasped as if in supplication.*) I said *all*!

JASON. Don't make him any madder than he *is*!

NICKI. I *refuse* to *grovel* before this man!

JASON. Oh, *please*! Just *humor* him a little! . . . Darling — ? . . . Monica — ? . . . Nicki — ?

NICKI. Why, Jason! (*drops to knees beside him*) You really *care*!

JASON. I know. All at once—I don't *need* a classy "Monica Kingsley" in my life! All I want is a nice little *Nicki* to hug!

NICKI. (*embraces him*) And you've *got* her—for life!

NAOMI. There! What did I tell you!

T.B. Enjoy your moment! When my *lawyers* get through with all of you, you won't be able to see each other except on *visitors'* day!

DOUG. You're talking *jail*?!

JASON. But we haven't committed a *crime*—?!

NICKI. (*with less assurance*) . . . *Have* we—?

T.B. (*glowing with triumph*) For starters, how about *malpractice*?! . . . *Unlawful detention*?! . . . *Conspiracy*?! . . . *Fraud*?! . . . *Terrorism*?! . . . And *indecent exposure*?!

VONGA. (*weakly*) The *Shriners* didn't mind . . .

T.B. Kingsley—you've totaled your last profit! Procter—you've taken your last pulse! Lavinia—Monica—*whatever* your name is—What *do* you do, anyhow?

NICKI. (*miserably*) I'm a dental hygienist.

T.B. (*with a chilling smile*) Well, *you're* going to find out what it's *really* like to live hand-to-mouth!

JASON. (*comes to his feet*) Now, *that's* going *too* far! Okay, so *I* don't measure up to the corporate image—but you're not going to mouth off like that to the woman I love!

DOUG. (*still on knees*) *That's* telling him, Jason!

NAOMI. Right on!

VONGA. Punch his lights out!

JASON. Darn right I will! (*takes step toward T.B., but stops on:*)

NICKI. (*grabbing his arm and jumping up*) Darling, no! You're in enough trouble already—don't add assault and battery to the list! . . . Much as he *deserves* it!

T.B. I *deserve* the treatment I've received here tonight?! For *what*, may I ask?

NICKI. For browbeating your employees! For ruling the company by *fear*! For making up stupid rules in areas that are none of your damned business! For making people wear three-piece wool suits in *July*!

OTHERS EXCEPT T.B. (*shake fists at him*) *Yeah!*

T.B. Well, I'm *going* to have you all arrested, *regardless*! And *how* do you intend to *stop* me?!

(*And POOPSIE steps in behind him via* K.L., *en route to hall door, senses the tension, turns her head, reacts, stops, and:*)

POOPSIE. (*bewildered and pleased*) *Alvin!*

T.B. (*whirls, sees her, shrieks in shock:*) *Poopsie!*

OTHERS. "*AL-VIN—*"?!

T.B. (*whirls to face them, wide-eyed with fear*) She's lying! She's lying, I tell you!

POOPSIE. (*moving toward him, curiously*) Of *course* you're Alvin!

T.B. I've never seen this woman before in my life!

POOPSIE. Silly, of *course* you have! Would I be going to *Bermuda* tomorrow with a *stranger*?

T.B. (*one last-ditch try*) We're *not* going to Bermuda tomorrow!

POOPSIE. (*pouts*) But I washed my *hair*!

JASON. (*as he and others come out of shock, and start putting it together*) The quiz show!

NICKI. The false beard and glasses!

NAOMI. It's M&M's corporate *image*!

DOUG. T.B. *Murdock* wouldn't *dare* be seen competing for prizes on TV!

JASON. No *wonder* he got so excited when he heard me shout "Poopsie"!

T.B. (*sags, a beaten man*) Oh, damn—oh, rats—oh, what's the use!

NAOMI. My-oh-my, just wait until *Mrs.* Murdock finds out about Poopsie!

JASON. Now, hold on—*he* may be a *stinker*—but *no* one likes an *informer!*

T.B. That's—most generous of you, Jason.

JASON. (*shrugs it off modestly*) Guy's gotta draw the line *somewhere* . . .

T.B. But it is *also* most *unnecessary.* (*when ALL look his way:*) There *isn't* any Mrs. Murdock!

DOUG. But—I've *seen* her—she's at *all* the company events—?!

JASON. Me, too!

T.B. (*shakes head*) *That* lady is my sister Tillie! She was just helping her bachelor brother—she doesn't get out very much. Let's be honest—*who'd* ever marry an old grouch like *me*?

NAOMI. Oh . . . you're not so bad . . .

T.B. Really?

NAOMI. Underneath the starched collar and crusty hide, I mean. Why, when you were screaming and fainting and carrying on—you were downright *cute!*

T.B. Why, Mrs. Schuyler!

NAOMI. *You* can call me "Naomi".

T.B. Naomi . . .

DOUG. (*the only one still on his knees*) Does this mean I can get *up*?

POOPSIE. (*moves to him*) Of course you can, Douggie! Here, let me help you!

DOUG. (*"Bogart" again in* another *famous line:*) Go ahead—you'd be doing me a favor!

POOPSIE. (*assists him up; then, huskily, nearly touching noses with him:*) I'd do *anything* to get those Letters of Transit!

DOUG. (*embraces her*) Ilsa!

POOPSIE. (*embraces him*) Oh, Rick! (*They kiss.*)

T.B. (*the only one at sea*) *What* letters of transit?

NAOMI. Don't you go to the movies?

T.B. I've always been too busy.

NAOMI. Well, don't worry. I've got *Casablanca* on videotape—we can watch it on the VCR—at *my* place . . .

T.B. But what about *Bermuda*?!

POOPSIE. (*breaking out of kiss finally*) Gee, I don't know exactly how to *say* this, but—well, what with meeting Douggie and all—well—

NAOMI. Uh . . . *I've* never been to Bermuda . . .

T.B. Naomi! Do you mean—*would* you—?

NAOMI. If my boss will give me the weekend off. . . ?

JASON. Hell, *I'll* be in *Connecticut*! Who's going to take my *phone* messages?

VONGA. *Vonga* can answer phone!

NICKI. There! It's all solved!

DOUG. And it'll serve your callers right!

NAOMI. Well, look, it's been a long evening—before anyone goes *anywhere*—who'd like a little *grub*?

VONGA. (*makes face*) Yuck! (*hides head under tablecloth again*)

JASON. She means *food*, not the *insect* larva! (*looks at NAOMI*) At least, I *hope* she does—?!

NAOMI. (*mysteriously, like a temptress*) Come into the kitchen and see. . . ! (*crooks her finger, slowly exits K.R., followed—in order—by T.B., DOUG, POOPSIE, NICKI and JASON; these last two pause for:*)

JASON. Vonga, you *can't* stay like *that* all weekend—?!

VONGA. (*straightens up*) Why?

JASON. Well, among *other* things, isn't it a little *boring*?

NICKI. Jason, she doesn't *have* to have a boring weekend. She can invite some *friends* over!

VONGA. Vonga *like* that. . . ! Is all right?

JASON. Well, of *course* it is! Make yourself right at home! (*He and NICKI exit* K.R., *and VONGA goes to phone, picks it up, dials "O" for the operator, and then:*)

VONGA. (*on phone*) Hello, please? . . . Operator? Ah, good ! . . . What is Area Code for Bronx Zoo — ? (*and as she stands there, smilingly awaiting a reply —*)

THE CURTAIN FALLS

End of Show

SPECIAL CASTING NOTE

A colleague asked me, after reading this manuscript, if I'd intended to have the role of Vonga played by a *black* actress, taking into account where her foster-parents had discovered her. And I explained something to him about *all* my plays, inclusive, from HERE LIES JEREMY TROY some 20 years ago to this one, my latest:

Race has *never* been a casting-factor in my shows. It's never mentioned, cited or recommended one way or the other. People are people, and if a group wished to do an all-black "JEREMY" or an all-Chinese SAVING GRACE or an all-Choctaw KISS OR MAKE UP, or whatever, they'll find that the basic *humanity* of the characters transcends *any* racial boundaries, and the plays will work just as well *whatever* race does them.

So if you wish to, say, do ONE TOE IN THE GRAVE with a white cast and a black Vonga, fine. Or a black cast and a white Vonga, fine. Or a white Jason, a Chinese Nicki, a Polynesian Doug, a Navajo T.B., a black Naomi, an Eskimo Poopsie, and an Aztec Vonga — go right ahead. People are people, and casting-calls for any of my shows are wide open to *all* comers. If you consider that *every* race has people in it who are tall, short, good, bad, fat, thin, refined, gross, bright, stupid, lovable and laughable, you'll see that it doesn't matter a particle. All the theatre has *ever* asked of an eager aspirant is: Have you got *talent*?! And that's all *I* ask, too.

JACK SHARKEY
November 1985

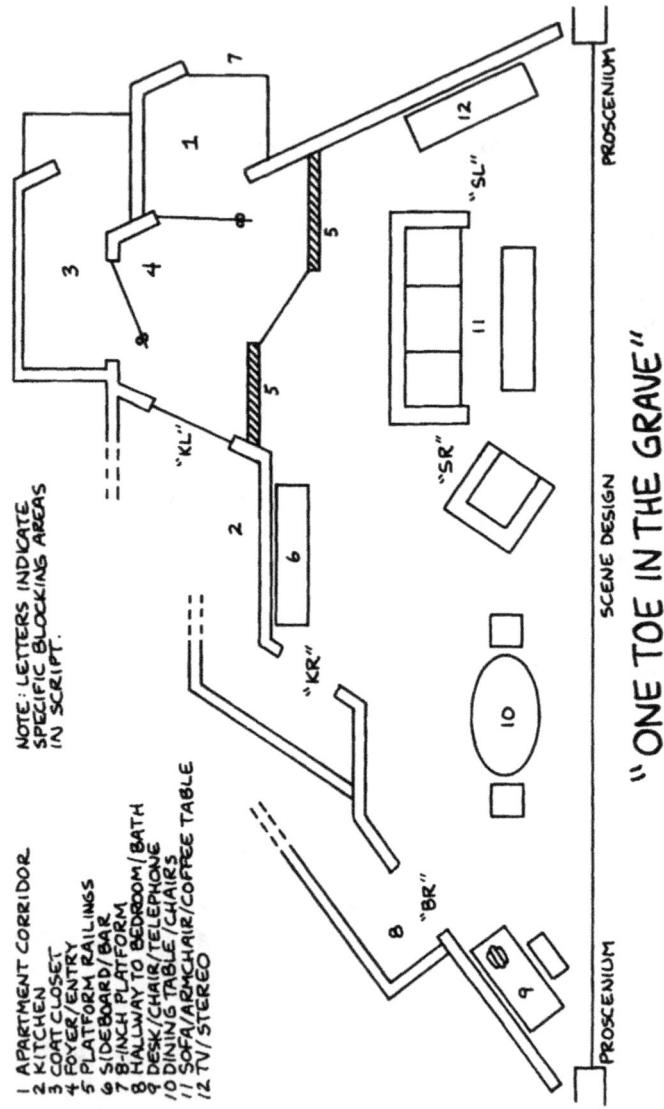

NOTE: LETTERS INDICATE
SPECIFIC BLOCKING AREAS
IN SCRIPT.

1 APARTMENT CORRIDOR
2 KITCHEN
3 COAT CLOSET
4 FOYER/ENTRY
5 PLATFORM RAILINGS
6 SIDEBOARD/BAR
7 8-INCH PLATFORM
8 HALLWAY TO BEDROOM/BATH
9 DESK/CHAIR/TELEPHONE
10 DINING TABLE/CHAIRS
11 SOFA/ARMCHAIR/COFFEE TABLE
12 TV/STEREO

PROSCENIUM

PROSCENIUM

SCENE DESIGN

"ONE TOE IN THE GRAVE"

MUSIC USE NOTE

Licensees are solely responsible for obtaining formal written permission from copyright owners to use copyrighted music in the performance of this play and are strongly cautioned to do so. If no such permission is obtained by the licensee, then the licensee must use only original music that the licensee owns and controls. Licensees are solely responsible and liable for all music clearances and shall indemnify the copyright owners of the play(s) and their licensing agent, Samuel French, against any costs, expenses, losses and liabilities arising from the use of music by licensees. Please contact the appropriate music licensing authority in your territory for the rights to any incidental music.

IMPORTANT BILLING AND CREDIT REQUIREMENTS

If you have obtained performance rights to this title, please refer to your licensing agreement for important billing and credit requirements.